Twists and Turns
Tale of an African Intellectual

Jonathan Tim Nshing

Langaa Research & Publishing CIG
Mankon, Bamenda

Publisher:

Langaa RPCIG
Langaa Research & Publishing Common Initiative Group
P.O. Box 902 Mankon
Bamenda
North West Region
Cameroon
Langaagrp@gmail.com
www.langaa-rpcig.net

Distributed in and outside N. America by African Books Collective
orders@africanbookscollective.com
www.africanbookcollective.com

ISBN: *9956-726-77-X*

1

S weat freely rolled down Newit's wrinkled face, as he sat at the table in his cubicle of an office. It rolled freely over the scars of his forehead – acquired years ago in a fall from a coconut tree. It was a hot Friday afternoon, and the leaves of the guava tree rustled outside his window in the hot sun. Newit's air conditioner had gone bad, and the university authorities had not yet sent someone to repair it.

Professor Newit's secretary, Shuila, was doing some work at her outmoded typewriter, left behind by the out gone French administration of the university. Professor Newit Anatole Lobe waited restlessly, his hands propping up his jaws as if they were about to fall off, for Mrs. Shuila Wang to finish. Having been his private secretary for some thirty years, she was accustomed to his impatience.

Shuila had cohabitated with his fiancé, Mr. Wang, a worker in the Department of Health, who died a year ago in a ghastly motor accident while going home to visit his family in the province. Mr Wang had for long been promising Shuila they were going to do the church wedding she so desired. Then he died without ever fulfilling the promise. This is what Prof. Newit was thinking about, about how life could be so cruel to some people, like Shuila. Like himself, he remembered how his wife had left him some twenty years ago with their only son, Mandala. As Newit remembered what Emeline had done to him in spite of all he had done for her, he was warmly tapped on the shoulder by Mrs. Shuila, announcing that Newit's Senate report was ready for him to have a glance at it.

1

Newit took the report and quickly dispatched Shuila to make him some coffee, forgetting he had vowed never to take coffee when it was hot, a habit he developed while as an undergraduate at Columbia University because it was fashionable there. But back home, he really doubted if he needed coffee given the hot climate. While he was still reading, Shuila returned with the cup of coffee, made from a local brand grown in the South Western region of the country, and three cubes of sugar. She handed him the cup of coffee with a broad smile. Newit remarked that Shuila was fast aging and hardly resembled the young energetic woman who had been assigned to him thirty years ago. Before Newit could finish the Senate report, which he had to draw up and present as the Senate's new rapporteur – replacing Prof. Lanston of Canadian nationality who had been in the university for the past twenty-five years and had gone on retirement back home –, he realised it was already 4:30 p.m. and he was doing overtime Shuila had already left. He hurriedly put the report alongside other documents and books into his ancient light grey brief case and hurried out of the office, putting on his jacket in the process.

The National University of Cameon better known by its acronym of NUC was founded in the early 1960s when the country just obtained independence. It consisted of five faculties, with about twenty departments. The administration of the university at that time was of entirely French nationals, with few Cameonese being assistant lecturers, just fresh from the Sorbonne or Aix-en-Provence and many other French higher institutions of learning. The campus of the university was fairly large, contained a library that was the best in Central Africa as well as its medical school known as the University Centre of Medicine and Health Science (UCMHS)

2

that competed only with others in Nigeria, Kenya and other Anglophone countries. The university was located along the major drive way into the capital city, Banta from the Western part of the country, situated some fifteen kilometres away from the city centre.

Newit had been teaching in this university for the past thirty years and for all this length of time he only became Head of Department in the Department of Government for the past five years. He filled in a gap that was created by the death of Professor Nguele Tene, the first national to have occupied such a position since the creation of NUC, to the embarrassment of Andre Delores, who was in that position as acting Head of Department. Delores had a Ph. D in public policy and who was attaché to the French Embassy in Banta. Newit finally grabbed the position to the embarrassment of Dr. Dolores, who immediately resigned his post at the French Embassy and left for home, insinuating that he could not imagine losing to an African pseudo-intellectual from some goddamn university in America.

Newit's five years at the head of the Department had not been a bed of roses as he constantly faced stiff opposition from his francophone colleagues, given the fact that he was English speaking, from the erstwhile British part of the country. His only friend in the Department, to whom he turned, was Dr. Ganta Luc, also French speaking, who like Newit had pursued his studies in the USA at the University of California at Los Angeles (UCLA). There were altogether seven members of staff and all of them shared a single office, in which they competed for space, with the rising piles of office stationary. There were also four chairs that were supposed to serve the seven of them. Only Newit had the privilege of the semblance of an air conditioned office.

3

It was a fine morning at NUC, a few days after Newit presented the Senate report, with the sun's rays streaming in through the window. Newit as usual was already in his office, when Shuila came in.

"Good morning, Doctor. Hope you had a nice sleep last night."

Newit retorted by reminding Shuila that he had told her to call him by his first name. "Morning, Shuila. How many times am I going to tell you to call me by my first name? Besides how's your daughter doing? I learnt she was involved in a cycling accident last evening."

"Yes, she was. She was rushed to St. Patrick's Clinic and the doctor says the fracture she sustained is a minor one and that she'll be fine by Wednesday."

With those words, Shuila excused herself intimating that she had some work to do. Left alone now in the office, Newit began to think what the week was going to look like for him. It was still Monday and he was thinking about getting a leave of about one month to visit his physician abroad for a routine medical check. Newit was already aging and had to take good care of his health, for his 59 years of existence, he had never been as concerned about his health as he had been for the last three years. His diabetes was under control and did not pose any peculiar problem to him now, but he still needed the medical check, just in case…

Newit mused himself when he heard a light tap at the door and before he had time to say "come in" Ganta was already half way through the room whose floor was covered with a Turkish rug that had lost its colour and originality and was nothing but threadbare now.

"Morning, Prof.," uttered Ganta.

"Morning, Ganta. I called your home yesterday evening and was told by your wife that you hadn't returned yet," Newit said.

"So how was the symposium? Was Professor Ben Flank from Georgetown in attendance?"

"We met on the opening day, thereafter, lost contact," responded Ganta. He was a man of composure known throughout the department for his wit and was so fondly liked by Newit. He handed some copies of the presentations that were made at "the International Symposium on Conflicts and Conflict Resolutions in Central Africa" that held at the Amadou Bello University, Zaria in Nigeria. Newit put on his horn-rimmed glasses to have a look at the pile of papers before him, as Ganta left to catch up with a class on political anthropology; he had with third year students at E- Block Amphitheatre.

Newit was reading through what he had just written down on an A4 paper for Shuila to type, which read thus:

Professor Newit Anatole
HOD, Department of Government
National University of Cameon
March 13

The Rector,
Via the Dean,
Faculty of Law and
Government,
National University of
Cameon

Sir,
Subject: **SICK LEAVE NOTIFICATION**

It is a pleasure for me once again to write to you, this time around to seek for permission to take a month long sick leave abroad to have a routine medical check.

I do intend to leave by March 20th and to be back by April 20th, I have already transferred my departmental responsibilities to my assistant Dr. Ganta.

While waiting for your eventual approval of this application, I remain grateful for your collaboration.

Yours Sincerely,

Newit Anatole.

This application brought to Newit's mind, memories of things past and those still in the offing. Newit had to spend his sick leave in the United States, and that is where his ex-wife was with his son. Newit bluffed and heard himself saying "shit", though he hated using that filthy word. He decided to think about something better. Newit after much consideration made up his mind that he had to visit his village prior to his departure abroad. It was about a year now since

6

he had been home, and he last went home when he lost his younger sister Magdeline and each time when he thought about her, fresh tears came to his eyes.

It was the following Saturday that Newit, spent his first night where he was born in his own house built on a plot that was given him by his late father. Only his paternal aunt was at home, his nieces and nephews had all gone to the farm. Newit' s aunt clutching onto a locally made staff, covered with calf skin, came in with a bowl of lukewarm water, and bar of soap for his brother's son to wash his face.

"Ne" called out his aunt, she abbreviated Newit's name because of her inability to pronounce it.

"Yes, Ma," came an automatic response from Newit. "What are you still doing in bed at this hour of the day, when your age mates are already on their second cups of wine in the village square? I had a bad night; Newit said as he drew off the blanket from his body and took the bowl of water from his aunt. He washed his face and had a shave while his eighty two year old aunt left the room to prepare him something to eat.

Breakfast this morning consisted of pounded cocoyams accompanied by a soup made up of boiled, mashed garden eggs, with some smoked fish. After Newit had his breakfast, he decided to have a stroll round the village to visit his kin, old time friends especially his mates in primary school, many of whom already boasted of at least two wives to as many as ten.

It was around 7:00 pm that Newit finally reached home after having made a round of the village, but he came back home with a heavy heart. What made him sad was the fact that contrary to what he thought, that his friends were doing fine, he was surprised to learn that many had died and he met

7

only their widows and children. He however had a nice time with the village head, a long time friend of his, who briefed him about the latest happenings in the village of Ntui.

Ntui was a small village of about four thousand inhabitants located in the Western slopes of Bakata Highlands of the North Western Region of the country. The village though remote was linked to the nearest major town some fifty-seven kilometres away by a well tarred road a gift by the Dutch government. Ntui had however produced one of the brightest brains in the country, that is him, when he thought over this at least this was what the village chief claimed, he mused to himself.

When Newit arrived home that evening, the whole family was already back from their various farms. He refused food that evening and had an early night because he had to travel back to Banta the next morning to proceed to the U.S city of Atlanta, that was the new haven for middle class African Americans and which was the home town of most of Newit's University days friends, among which was his long time friend at Columbia state university. Dr. Greg Burger, who owned one of the best private clinics in the city, with whom Newit was going to stay during his stay in the states.

2

Prof. Newit was in class with first year undergraduates and this morning he taught Introduction to Comparative Politics. The students though still naughty, interested Newit so much because they reminded him of his student days at Columbia University when he himself was an undergraduate, how he could hardly get a word from what the professor was saying. To him, the man was speaking through his nostrils and was more of a laughing stock to Newit and his other African friend Koffi from Ghana, who had never been used to such. He also found himself being the laughing stock of these students, who thought he was using the white man's accent, though he wanted and tried to be heard and appear African in his speech. He thought what a mockery the whole exercise was, because he knew that he was not original neither white in speech nor totally black, but some caricature and a half baked African intellectual trying to sound white. There was nothing he could do about it, what goes round comes round he found himself agreeing with the author of this saying whoever the author was. Whenever Newit came out from such classes, he felt so exhausted and worn out to the extent that he thought of giving up everything and quietly retire back to his village, where no such stress existed. After all he had made some modest savings throughout his career.

Newit often decried the catechist's stipend of a salary he was paid in spite of his level of education. When he thought of what his colleagues in other places earned, he almost grew mad. It was due more to the fact that he considered his job as rendering a service to his nation that made him stay on. The money he earned while delivering part time lectures in Israel and Britain were four times what he earned at NUC. The government had reduced civil servants to mere puppets and only those who could dance to the tune of those in power lived luxurious lives. Newit had seen 'soya' but had sadly let it pass him by, something, some of his colleagues could not let go. Three years ago, he was appointed second Deputy Minister of the Interior, but he to the surprise of everyone declined the post.

At times, Newit often feels that he should have accepted the post, because refusing it would not help things either. However, something deep within him at the same time keeps telling him that was the best thing he ever did in his whole life. That is refusing in spite of the juicy emoluments to mess up with the cycle of chronic corruption that had gripped the whole country. Newit had all along his life been guided by a strong moral code and this was well known.

Within the University community, in fact some of his colleagues mockingly referred to him as Mr. Christ, they meant that if he claimed to be a righteous man then he was not meant for this world and especially that it was a mistake for him to have been born a Cameonese, because being a Cameonese was synonymous to "you chop, I chop," and everyone understood it perfectly without being necessarily told. Children were born and grew up in the system; Newit remembered a saying in his native tongue that said, a hen cannot give birth to a kitten. At times Newit felt like just giving up, but he felt he still had young minds to groom, that there was still much to live for.

The next Sunday, Newit decided to go to church as usual, this particular Sunday, the church was full as a matchbox that

Newit could hardly breathe. But the pastor was loud enough for anyone without ear problems to get him. Rev. Peter Brawn had been in the country for the past twenty years and understood perfectly what was happening in the country. People had almost forgotten that he was, a German, who came to Cameon as missionary to work for the Cameon Baptist Mission, known for short as CBM. Rev Braun's sermon this morning was centred on "the obligation to work" and was drawn from the Book of 2 Thessalonians 3:6-13. In this portion of the Bible, "the Apostle Paul was emphasizing that lazy people should not be allowed among the Christian Community because he himself Paul and his fellow–workers did everything not to constitute a burden to others" Rev. Braun drawled in English, which he spoke with a heavy German accent.

"Paul insisted that the Christians of Thessalonica had to continue to work hard but at the same time had to continue helping those who were less privileged." Rev. Braun drew an illusion to what was happening in the country, in which nobody felt the obligation to work, "nobody worked because it was his duty, but because, he expected his pay by the end of the month, no matter the circumstance. He paused to clear his throat before he continued.

"We have all become a disgrace to God's kingdom and are not worthy of the name Christians because we have lost the purpose of Christianity," said Rev. Braun.

"You cannot be a leader without leading an exemplary life, you have to set the pace." Being a Christian means that you have to help your less fortunate brother next door, not pouring all the money you have on the church. Remember our God is not a poor God, but one who has more than enough and gives to us abundantly and in the same token

11

expects us to do same. We have all refused to do our work because we want to be bribed, who are we fooling? Is it man or God? Brother, sister, I call on you today to reflect on how you do your work, do you defraud people? If so, your faith is dead faith in fact you are a dead man. If all of us could just do our work as we are supposed to, refuse the temptation by Satan through the bribes, truly this country would change for the better. And the angels in heaven would all give glory to God. As you go home today, I want you to think over this, God helping us that we would do our work however humble it may be and make things right with God. May God bless you" Everyone went home that day in a reflective mode

Monday was a most busy day for Newit and all members of the departure as they were receiving some guest from Canada, who came to negotiate an exchange program with NUC. The delegation that was led by Prof. Jean Clavier included nine other members.

Université de Montréal was interested in helping NUC to set up a viable school of Government and to provide staff as well as logistics. This program had been negotiated by Newit. It had been his lifelong dream to see a school of government come to function in the country and he felt elated as his dream was about to be realized. He together with the rest of his staff had a working session with the Canadian delegation. An agreement was reached between Université de Montréal and NUC for the exchange of students as well as teachers between the two universities beginning from the next year, every second semester for the whole semester. At the end of semester, the host university was to set the exams. After the delegation left to visit some tourist sites in the country, Newit and Ganta had some time to themselves and decided to have lunch together at the university staff restaurant. Newit was served some ripe plantains with chicken sauce while Ganta preferred cassava paste with roasted fish, a typical dish of the natives of Banta. While they were busy savouring their meals, Newit received a phone call from Diane, his new lover, who was fondly referred to by friends as Lady Diana. Newit had been having an affair with Diane for about a year now, though at the beginning, he had been reluctant given the disappointment he had from Emeline, who had deserted him while they were still in the States in favour of a white automobile salesman. Since then, he had dealt with women very cautiously. Ganta was bewildered as to why Newit could not take the chance, now that the memory of Emeline was gone. He couldn't help but listen to the conversation between Newit and Diane over Newit's cellular phone, at least to what Newit was saying.

"Honey, how's your day? Hope the flu's over?" asked Diane.

"I guess I'm as strong as a horse now," came the reply from Newit.

"Newit, you know it's been quite some time, we haven't had lunch together, not to talk of you touching me, what's the problem? Is it that I'm not as good as Emeline was? I feel horrible".

"Take it calmly, you know I'm too busy now, but I'll make out some time to be with you over the weekend. Is that okay by you?" Newit tried to sound reassuring, while Diane pressed on.

"Busy, busy, busy, is all you say, or you want to tell me you're the busiest man on earth? I'm not surprised, you have never loved me."

It was with those words that Diane dropped the phone, to the utter consternation of Newit. He took a deep breath,

the thunderous applause of his audience from the amphitheatres to colloquium hall but this one was different.

PAM launched its campaign on all fronts and was set for the conquest, Newit shouted out his lungs from soap boxes, words of inspiration to the youths, to whom destiny seemed to have particularly hated from one corner of the country to the other. Yes PAM brought in a difference to the game of politics, people for the first time in their lives, realized that some political parties at least from soap boxes had a different vision as to how things were to be done. The economy was down and subject to foreign machinations of every imaginable kind, the youths were out there in the streets hopeless disease had been accepted as a permanent companion, in conformity with the maxim that "if you can't beat them, join them". Unemployment had reached epidemic proportions, in every family of about ten persons of working age, eight were unemployed. Corruption was the only word that could win or defeat any other opponent by a hundred percent in any election. In fact, rules had been set for the game and everybody understood them perfectly; a cab driver was not told that he had to put a five hundred francs note or coin in his chest pocket, for ready removal whenever he was intercepted by the traffic police. Moreover, these uniformed officers had through the practice of constant collection received the booty with such expertise that even the most prudent observer was not able to see. Back there in their offices only those who could return to the office with a handsome harvest for the boss were sure to be sent out next time. There was talk that the government was waging a stiff anti- corruption battle, campaign after campaign came up and no sooner had it been set up that it died. Who was to blame, the government or the citizens?" It was difficult to say. The church had become a thriving business enterprise as the mainstream churches were caught in internal ramblings and consequently losing their membership to some money driven "Holy Ghost" preachers whose churches were nothing more than the preacher, his wife, children, relations, some few friends and job-seeking and marriage seeking young people.

These were the things PAM preached everywhere it went, but what was most fascinating in the whole matter, is the fact that PAM saw in this bleak picture, an illusory hope or as Newit believed real hope. If and only if the people gave them their support. These were the things that bothered Newit dressed in a grey British suit he bought when he was last in London as he mused about the image he saw in the dressing mirror of his bedroom. But he also made some sad observations, age was weighing hard on him, his hair had all gone grey on his head save for the smooth, ever advancing bald head. His somewhat potbelly had almost outgrown his coat and that rendered him a little uncomfortable. The wrinkles on his forehead were increasing in depth as well as in length, his once energetic jaws were drooping, he found it difficult to reconcile this image with that in the picture that hung from the niche at the head of his bed. The hard reality was that he was actually aging and nearing the end of his tether. "That is life", he heard himself saying and off to the great meeting he went.

3

The results had started coming in, the state owned Radio and Television channels were giving their own side of the story, to them the ruling party had grabbed most of the votes from the countryside and there was a similar tendency in the big cities. CNBN that stood for Cameonese National Broadcast Network also reported that PAM had made some impressive gains in the urban areas but was losing in the countryside. The newspaper, tabloids, foreign television and radio stations were giving a totally different picture from what CNBN gave. According to CNBN, the LPR of the President or better still the Chef was posed for a resounding 60% victory, while PAM was currently retaining about 25% of the vote while the other four parties combined were trailing behind with about 15%. As the counting continued, it became clear to everyone that contrary to what was said over the state media, PAM was heading for a landslide victory in all parts of the country, even in the president's village, which was considered a traditional fief of LPR. There were reports especially in the papers of the stuffing and mysterious disappearance of ballot boxes in the president's province in apparent retaliation to encroachments from PAM into places of which it wasn't supposed to. There were reports of abductions, arbitrary arrests, detentions, and even murder in some cases. The whole country was thrown into panic, as no one no longer knew what was happening, there were reports to the fact that the President had fled, the military was in the streets instituting real martial law. A curfew was declared in all the major towns. There was real fear and in the midst of all these, the government was as silent as death, it as if in agreement with the saying that government does not speak but acts. In essence, life came to a halt. It was in the midst of all these that election results were made public. They came like a time bomb that had all along kept silent and just waited for one of its connecting cords to be pulled off. The curfew was immediately after the publication of the results extended over the whole country, a state of emergency was immediately decreed in the capital Banta, and de Gaullesville, the second largest town. It did not surprise many when the state-owned radio announced on that fateful evening that in the final results LPR had grabbed sixty five percent, PAM fifteen and the other smaller parties twenty percent. Some cried foul while some offered cocktails and threw parties, the other political leaders seemed to have been injected with an overdose of anaesthesia, for they appeared to sleep eternally. Things went on fast, Newit was more than frightened, he thought to himself, how those who said politics was not, made for intellectuals were right. Where was his place finally, in the classroom or on soap boxes? For he felt he had done more than enough with the chalk and all along, he had fooled himself that politics was an honourable game. He had failed as PAM's campaign strategist.

These were the thoughts that preoccupied Newit's mind as he was ushered out of the poorly lit mosquito infested cell to a foul stinking flushing toilet that had been blocked by faeces newspaper shreds that served as toilet tissue. He did not understand, whether it was a deliberate act from the prison guards to enjoy how wonderful it was for V.I.P prisoners like him to defecate on themselves. When he was left to himself inside the filthy stinking toilet, just from what he saw, he decided to keep his shit for much longer and instantly felt relieved. He was ushered back to the hole of a cell which he shared with fifteen other members of his party by the horrid looking warden, who was whopping out tuberculosis molecules from his tobacco corrupted lungs. He was a man of great built with a chest as broad as the ear of an elephant and was known around the prison yard as the Hangman. He commanded Newit to continue moving as a confident captain does in warfare in which he was confident to win in some broken French "Messieurs l'opposerant, vite tu perd mon temps, ce n'est que le commencement". He was thrown back into the cell with such jerking force that he found it hard to distinguish if it was a kick or a shove that he got on his butt. He joined the rest for a collective bemoaning of their fate, how they survived in that cell, only God alone knows, fifteen persons for two bug and flea infested flat mattresses with nothing to cover. To have two meals a day was a luxury if meals they were, a loaf of some stale bread with a cup of coloured sugarless water were enough for breakfast. Lunch constituted of weevil-infested rice and beans or was substituted by what was some strange mixture of corn stew popularly known as corn chaff. These meals were served sparingly and could be done in any order, some days in the morning and afternoon, then in some, morning and evening. Newit had at least received some honour from those with whom he cohabited. He was allowed one of the two mattresses to himself given his age and status; there was real African solidarity in this new world. One had to share whatever one had with the others including Bronchitis which soon began spreading from person to person in this cell. That was the royal treatment Newit and his friends tested and endured for two months, two days, twenty two minutes, Two persons who were with Newit in the same cell latter on made

31

the transition to the world beyond as a result of the incarceration of better still detention without trial.

When Newit finally got out from "Le Dragon" Prison, which was situated some fifteen kilometres in the outskirts of the capital, Diane was there together with Ganta to take him home. Newit and the others were released on bail as the legal proceedings against them were continuing. They had been accused of disturbing public peace and inciting the public to riot and for purported arms possession. Their prison term could last from anything to life imprisonment. The government had bowed to pressure from the international community especially the donor countries and organizations. These countries and human rights groups contended that up to a thousand people had been killed and more than two hundred unaccounted for in the post electoral violence.

When Diane saw how pale-looking Newit was with his overgrown beard resembling that of some Maghreb herdsman, tears immediately came to her eyes. Ganta was in more control of his emotions, for that was all he could do to demonstrate his manhood in the face of the scenario that was unfolding in front of him.

"Oh my God! Newit, you look terrible. Are you feeling well?" asked Diane.

"Diane, I'm fine," replied Newit with a straight face as Diane fell on him and burst into more tears. Ganta spoke this time.

"Nice to see you after such trying moments."

"Thank you Ganta, I know you'll always stand by me," Newit responded.

"Ganta continued, "We've been here, Diane and I, practically every day but these lunatics wouldn't allow us to see you. I guess you must have been receiving the notes we struggled to smuggle in. You must have learnt that that filthy–looking Garba is with them, he even accepted a cabinet post."

"Thank you once for your concern, at least I learnt of that in the cell, things like these happen."

He had hardly finished his sentence when Diane slowly pulled away from him in order to have a second look at him as Ganta stepped forward to receive Newit's bag of personal effects from an almost hunch backed prison senior constable. The superintendent of the prison suddenly appeared at the doorway and told Newit arrogantly in English; "

"You are free to leave, but only make sure you don't come here again because here there are no students to shout to but commands to obey."

Ganta pulled open the door of the passenger seat of his Mitsubishi car for Diane and did the same for Newit who sat at the back seat alone and was left to his thoughts. The ride home that afternoon was exceedingly slow, as cars of every imaginable make were crowded into two files, those going towards the central town and those coming from that direction. This situation was exacerbated by the bumpy nature of the road, whose tar was gradually wearing down giving way to potholes some of which were up to a foot deep. Even the traffic lights were no better, one had to strain their eyes in order to see what lights read, they could switch from one sign to the other without you noticing given the fact that the bulbs were no better than torch lamps whose batteries had worn out. The middles lanes as well as the sidewalks had most unusual and fascinating attractions. There were heaps of household refuse on them as well as the carcasses of cheap vehicles from Europe, which helped to transform these heaps into roadside junkyards. There were some roundabouts that had been created by the emergence and invasion of these areas by these heaps of dirt that resembled the pyramids found in Egypt. Dogs, mad people, destitute as well as children could be seen scavenging inside these heaps in order to pick up those few items such as expensive wine bottles and food leftovers from generous dining tables, which by their estimation had been thrown here by accident. These persons competed with an impressive colony of flies for attention. The smell of these heaps of dirt as well as the ever-increasing heat nauseated Newit and in the midst of all those things, he drifted slowly to sleep if and only if he could sleep forever.

The next day, Newit in the company of Diane was at the L'Hôpital Les Bon Soigneurs" Dr. Ntan who studied and practised medicine in the U.K and had recently returned home, was also a friend of Newit's. It was at his clinic that Newit mostly consulted. After the examination, the doctor told him;

"Your sugar level has increased significantly to over 130, I guess you have to go back to the insulin injection which you so much dread. But I'll want to assure you that there's not much to worry about".

"So Doctor, had it been that, I spent up to two months in that Godforsaken place, maybe I wouldn't be here talking with you?" asked Newit as anger began rising in him as he thought about what he had just gone through. But he was calmed down by Dr. Ntan, who sounded reassuring.

"You need not worry as I've already told you, just try to take these medications as well as the insulin injection and then we'll see what we can do"

Newit was already up as he exchanged a fraternal handshake with the doctor who too was already up and handed him the prescription.

"Thank you, Doctor." Said Newit.

"You don't have to, what are friends for?" retorted Dr. Ntan.

"See you in a fortnight," he went on.

Diane was in the lobby, reading a foreign woman's magazine. When she saw Newit, she immediately jumped up as if something had just bitten her on the seat.

"Honey what has the doctor said?" she asked as she stood perplexed and rooted to the ground to the utter consternation of the nurse receptionist. Newit immediately dismissed her fears.

"Everything's fine, at least I'm still alive" and with those words he took Diane's small hands into his and looked her straight in the eye. Thereafter they proceeded to the hospital pharmacy.

With pressure from the international community and with the human rights organisations such as Human Rights Watch to investigate into the abuses that had taken place in the country during and after the elections, the government decided to drop the charges against Newit and his associates. Garba was already a member of government, with the not too enviable post of Minister Delegate in charge of Rural Development. Two of his other associates were given two other ministerial portfolios that were hardly even known to the public. With affairs having been patched up with the main opposition party in the country, the government was now set for the resumption of normal relations with foreign donor countries as well as organisations. These things no longer surprised Newit, he had learnt the hard way how things were done. He remembered the popular saying in the streets in Pidgin English "who come for loss" and that kind of comforted him. If Garba of all could do this to him, then

35

who did he really have to trust in this thing called politics? This is a man who came to him and practically begged him to join in the formation of a party and for him to offer his expert help, which he did and only for him to turn around and realized that he had been stabbed in the back. These memories were really sickening, the stomach could make people to become so mean, if it wasn't to 'chop', then why had Garba sold out, why did he abandon him in the prison when things got rough and up to now, he had received practically no word from him? Was it worth the salt for him to have joined? He doubted.

Diane spent the night at Newit's place; he really needed someone to comfort him, to give him the strength to go on, not to break up, for the pressure was too much. That night, Diane was dressed in a silk-laced nightgown that exposed almost every contour of her body. She was silhouetted against the light streaming out of the villa and had on a suede cap that resembled one of these Hollywood soap opera actresses. She held a glass of Baron de Lyons is in one hand while supporting her frame on a nearby pillar. Newit was in the garden sipping the same wine, which he diluted with syrup. He quickly finished his drink, precipitated by what he saw through Diane's nightgown that sent cold tremors down his spine and made him want to possess her forever. Diane was still a revelation to Newit. Her three children she had with Sam were all grown up and in faraway lands, that meant that she was entirely his, but he had completely made up his mind to marry her as she wanted. But Emeline's memory kept on haunting him, he thought of what might have happened to his son Mandala who was now twenty. It was now a very long time since he had last seen him. He was suddenly interrupted in his thoughts by Diane, who called out to him that it was already past ten and time to go to bed.

Some people say love is a feeling but for Newit, love was a language, for how could he explain what was happening to him now, his whole body was on fire, the rhythmic regularity with which Diane thrust herself into him was so overpowering that he was speechless, it was like he was hoodwinked as those soldiers were on the magical fruit in Tennyson's Lotus fruit. Diane was crying out "love me, love me Newit, I want you." Newit responded with equal measure as he showered Diane with a sea of kisses. By the early hours of the morning, Diane was cuddled up on Newit's body, her head rested on his chest and her dark hair spread out over her face and she looked so young and innocent that Newit felt guilty for having made love to her the way he did last night. This was the woman he did not want but ironically, it was she who had made him stay afloat, the way things happen still marvelled him. There was the world against him but here was his only soldier, a woman for that matter that fought off all his enemies. When he narrowed his eyes towards the wall clock that hung over the dressing mirror, it was already six-thirty and he was not happy, he had to begin this routine life every blessed day and that's why he prayed for many of such nights which he had just had with Diane. He decided to put on the radio to listen to what news it was that morning. Behold, he heard a communiqué from the President of the Republic's Civil Cabinet announcing an amnesty for all those who were involved in the post electoral violence. He sighed and thought what the president was up to. Later on that morning in his office, he received a sealed letter from Madam Shuila and when he opened it, he realized that it was from the Rector. That increased his curiosity; the adrenalin in his veins

37

increased and his heart thudded faster and ever missed some beats. He read through the note with all anxiety. He was needed at the Rector's office with immediate effect.

4

When he arrived at the chancellery, he did not go through the normal procedure that was at the entrance. The security person at the gate was already on his seat and sluggishly pulled open the glass door with much perplexity as if he had been fighting with himself to open or not to open the door. Newit threw it open himself with much ease as Oumarou, the guard shouted:

"Good Morning Doc," in a faltering voice. In return, he got a nod of the head from the profile that had just gone past him. Newit was already inside the lobby of the chancellery and passers–by as well as other workers who were leisurely seated in the lobby as if they had nothing doing looked on dumbfounded. He engaged the staircase with much agility; he glided up his hand on the baluster in the process as if without that he would fall back. The Rector's office was located in the fourth floor of the chancellery that had been christened by both students and teaching staff as "Court Militaire" this was because when you had a problem with the administration and were summoned by the chancellery, you had to start a new job search if you were a staffer or you had to try your luck out of the country, for you were refused admission in other state owned universities if you were a student in the country with just a phone call from your former university. As Newit alighted from the stairs of the fourth floor, he already contemplated the fate that awaited him. His feet felt like giving way below as he got into the Rector's secretariat. The Rector's private secretary was on seat as well as one other administrative assistant.

"Go--------- Good afternoon sir," stuttered Benjamin, for that was the name of the man. "Morning is the Rector in?" growled Newit as a sharp pain gripped the pit of his stomach.

"Yes Sir, he's waiting for you, you may go right in," as he gestured to the door that was made of Tropical mahogany, the other lady stared at Newit and momentarily stopped what she was doing and as if she'd seen some ghost. She was equally lost in a myriad of wild thoughts. Newit pushed open the door with much dexterity. Seated some seven metres form him was the Rector Dr. Ezekiel Goka, who was known throughout the campus for his quick temperament and could grab first prize with whoever when it concerned falling into fits of anger. Nevertheless, today, he seemed to be relaxed as he enjoyed the cold air that was generated by the brand new air conditioner that only he and his deputies had the privilege of enjoying. His office was a chapel when compared to Newit's cubicle. On his table were photographs of him, his two wives and some of his several children. Goka was known throughout Banta for his remarkable ability to keep two official wives, a battalion of concubines as well as their children all over the town. It was even said that he was a friend of the Chef and could continue staying in his post as long as one of his daughters continued servicing the groins of the president. The office was well furnished with a rug that must have cost a fortune, there was a section with sofas that were specially ordered from France as well as a television set put for the relaxation of Goka's guests, at the centre of the office hung a large beautifully decorated chandelier. Goka told Newit to come right in and pointed him the seat that was directly in front of him to sit. Goka drawled in the huskiest voice, Newit ever heard.

"Will you take some whisky?" Newit replied with a voice as flat as plywood:

"No," As Goka quickly realized that this was going to be a no-win situation, he tried on his intrigue,

"I called you up this afternoon with orders from the minister, I know you may want to ask, 'what for' but be a bit patient." Newit had never in his whole life been calm as he was today; he gave Goka a poignant stern look that sent shock waves down every nerve and veins in Goka. Goka appeared dull-eyed and decided to babble what he had to say as fast as possible and release himself and release himself from Judas' guilt.

"Newit I---I have instructions from hierarchy to inform you of your transfer from this institution to the West Cameon University at Frantwick, you will receive a formal letter to this effect as soon as possible. This therefore means that you have lost your post as HOD in this institution. I want to tell you that personally I don't have any ill-will against your person. You know I'm not that kind of person. You should contact the accounting officer for all your outstanding allowances. I wish you well in your new station."

Though Newit had expected such bad news, he was mortified in his seat as he sat rooted to the seat and prayed why he wasn't a spirit to disappear from the surface of the earth. He was unnerved and before Goka could realize it, he was already on his feet, he shot Goka a deadly look accompanied by the following words. "I kind of expected this, but did not imagine that it was going to be you. All the same, thank you for having succeeded at last to boot me out."

"But...... but, I...I did not..." Goka started off but did not land as if to say if you can't say the truth then ramble.

Newit did not wait to get the last wordings of Goka's aborted attempt at self-justification.

A sharp pain grabbed Goka's stomach and he gritted his teeth and cried out "this good-for- nothing son of bitch, what does he think he is up to, I've not yet started with him" with those words, he heaved a sigh of relieve and collapsed his bulk into the sofa as it almost gave way under him as he lit his Moroccan cigar to smack the pain.

The next day, Newit did not even bother to go to the University campus, he decided that before his formal dismissal letter would come, he would have already dismissed himself and so from the moment he left that good-for-nothing Rector's office, he was already unemployed. He decided to forget about the arrears that were owed him by both the government as well as the university. Fortunately for him, he had worked for long and within that length of time had saved enough that could keep him going comfortably till death. Having been also thrown out as Vice Secretary of PAM, he now realized what the world actually meant for him. Was God, a just God, if so where was he when all these things were happening to him? Newit had never in his whole life doubted his faith as he did presently but fortunately, he still had Diane. This woman, there was something magical about her, she had imposed herself on him and had done so effectively. Time is the best mediator, if not then how could one explain the fact that Newit had grown to love Diane in spite of himself and wanted her now like death. There was a mystery about women that Newit still had to decipher, "One woman leaves another comes, one breaks your heart the other mends it" what a vicious cycle, he thought. Newit's thoughts drifted from both Emeline and Diane to what had just happened to him the previous day. About his dismissal and punitive transfer from NUC to West Cameon University, he decided that for him to go to Frantwick, on demotion it would be better to stay at home. After all, he was not going to be evicted or forced to move out of his house too as his enemies could also want. He also decided that his teaching career had come to a precipitated end. Only two things now interested him now, one was that he had to formally wed Diane and two he had to spend the rest of his life out of this dirty game, politics as peacefully as possible. He was not to be subjected to the mean treatment he had so far received from people he thought were his friends.

5

The memory of what had happened to him, both the political victimization, blackmail from his fellow ex colleagues of PAM as well as his dismissal from the university had been conveniently forgotten. He had at last understood the writing on the wall, without having been taught. The best teacher, Newit now understood was experience. If you didn't experience something first hand you were like someone who had a box of fine gems in his hand but had never seen one. Now was time to forget about the past, "Let by-gones be by-gones", he had had more than a fair share of life's injustice. He had to forget about the past especially now because there was nothing there that made him a proud man. But he equally acknowledged to himself that one could never dissect oneself from the past, it lingers on in our lives perhaps to remind us of the fact that we are harboured on human foundations that are imperfect.

It had been over two months since Newit had last been to church or to his old time friend Rev Braun. He decided that he was going to pay him a visit that evening. Before he could finish ironing his dresses, that bright morning, something he was forced to do because Mrs. Gemun was sick and he had accorded her some rest till when she felt better, he heard the bell of the main door ring. He hurriedly plucked off the iron and put it away, got up and felt some pain around his waist, due to the fact that he had been bent for about an hour, sweat was on his forehead and his hands were equally sweaty before he had time to head towards the door, the bell rang again, this time persistently, Newit got angry as he approached the door, cursing whoever it was that had the audacity to disturb his peace. When he pulled open the door, he was so carried away in anger that he gave a stern look at Simon, Rev Braun's youngest son, who trembled out a tremulous:

"Good, Good morning Sir",

"Morning son, what brings you here early this morning? Is there anything the matter?" "My...my father says you should come just now", Simon panting succeeded to say. He was Braun's last son and Braun was so fond of him. He was around him all the time save when he was in school, this morning, he looked older than his eleven years Newit immediately understood that things were not well.

"You don't look your best my boy, is he ill or something?" Newit pressed softly as he narrowed his eyes on Simon's innocent face.

"Yes... Yes, he took ill last night and started coughing and mama tried to make him sleep but he wouldn't."

"Ok my boy you come right in, while I change into something more presentable". Newit hurriedly ran up the staircase as fast as his feeble legs could allow him go, while wondering what could have happened to his old friend. Though he knew that Rev. Braun often complained of rheumatism, he had never complained of any other illness, so this time it must be serious, he at last convinced himself. In about five minutes, he was back into the living room dressed in a light blue cashmere shirt impressively super imposed on blue-black pants; Newit looked twenty years younger though he was already closing in on sixty.

"Son, we can get going" Newit drawled as Simon woke up from his seat and whimpered; "un...uncle, my birthday is next week."

"Twelfth?" asked Newit.

"Yes…yes uncle, Simon gabbled in a silky voice as he pushed open the door. When they were outside and after Newit had keyed the door, he told Simon:

"Remind me over the weekend, you know I've a bad memory." as he gave his younger companion a broad smile as he got into the driver's seat of his car and then opened the passenger's door for Simon. He reversed the car out of the garage into the hot morning sun.

Rev Braun was wrapped up into a bundle of pain in bed when Newit arrived. He was ushered into Braun's bedroom by Hilda, Braun's eldest child. Helen was seated on Braun's bed and meticulously dipping a hand towel into a bowl of lukewarm water and compressing it on Braun's forehead. Braun's body was very hot and he was half-asleep and lay still while from time to time casting some hazy glances at his wife and his children who came into the room from time to time. He seemed to have momentarily lost memory and constantly called Helen, Maria which was his mother's name who had long died when he was still ten. When Helen saw Newit who had walked into the room almost stealthily, she began sobbing, Newit came round to the other side of the bed where Helen was seated and asked almost impatiently;

"How is he doing?"

"Mr Newit, my husband, is he going to die"? She succeeded to say in a faltering voice that was void of life.

"No, Helen, you should not say that, everything is going to be just fine. Have you already called the doctor?" he asked.

"No, he said we shouldn't call the doctor till when you come" Helen drawled.

"Ok. I'll call the doctor immediately" as he got out his Erickson cellular phone and dialled his friend Dr Ntan of Le

Bon Soigneur hospital. After he had made the call, Dr Ntan promised to be at the Mission yard as soon as possible. Word had already spread round the neighbourhood that Rev Braun was ill and a group of concerned parishioners was already gathering outside. After about three minutes, Braun opened his eyes very slowly as someone who was resurrecting and immediately asked in an almost inaudible voice if Newit had already come. Newit answered him;

"Reverend, I'm already here" Braun still lay motionless and after what seemed like a century drawled in the most unusual voice Newit had ever heard in his whole life;

"Ne….Newit, I….I called you here this morning to tell you…" he writhed his teeth in pain as if he was pricked by some unknown thing and continued;

"To tell you that I'm already going, you take care of my children; my will is with my lawyer Geo..rge Ballad."

Newit was listening patiently as his palpitation grew faster and faster, he held Rev. Braun's hands in his as if to tell Braun that though this was happening to him, he was not forgotten. Rev. Braun managed to tell his wife to call in all his seven children. They all rushed in, with tear stained eyes, while Newit told them to take heart and not to cry. Helen was already weeping uncontrollably as if Braun was already dead. Newit gestured to Hilda and her siblings to come round to the other side of the bed. When they were all gathered by the bedside, Braun managed to look up lamely at his children and said in a murmur;

"My….my children, I…I want you to know that I love you all…" He coughed out and continued as he clung harder to Newit's hands.

"Hil….Hilda" he managed to call out as Hilda answered instantaneously "Daddy".

"You know, you're my first child and I want you to be an example to your brothers and sisters and to the whole society as I and your mother have taught you, you should all obey your mother. The Bi…Bible says…" he didn't finish what he was about to say as he slipped into a coma.

The room was already invaded by some curious parishioners as Dr Ntan mingled and forced his way through the ever-increasing heads into the room. Newit told the parishioners to wait in the living room; the doctor put down his brief case and immediately removed his stethoscope, put it into his ears and placed the other end on Braun's bare chest and nodded to himself from what he read from the gauge. He also opened Braun's eye as well as his mouth as both Newit and Simon looked on with Newit man enough not to have cried like his other sister. Helen had already been taken out of the room by a group of women in order to calm her down.

"From what I see, his heart's failing and I suspect leukaemia a disease that attacks the blood and can lead to heart failure though I'll need to run some tests on him." Dr Ntan said as last after having examined Braun briefly for about five minutes. The ambulance attendants were already in the room with a stretcher as Rev. Braun was taken out from the room still in a coma into the waiting ambulance. In a few minutes the ambulance was off to the Le Bon Soigneur Hospital.

The next day, at about 5:00am in the morning, Rev. Braun was confirmed dead by Prof Atiri, who was called in by Dr Ntan from the Referral Hospital. It was a sad day in the neighbourhood of La Paroisse where the church was found. The sun had refused to shine and it was drizzling. The bells of the mission tolled at 6:00am that morning instead of the usual 5:30 am 30 minutes late and some parishioners had gone for morning meditation at that time, wondering what had happened that the bells had not been tolled, those who stayed back home heard the bells at 6:00 am and equally wondered why the church secretary was that late this morning. The whole parish was thrown into confusion, those who were on time for morning meditation were astonished to find that the pastor was not there, they wondered what must have kept him late at the personage, he was known throughout the whole parish for his punctuality. What must have happened this morning was the question on everyone's lips. Some guessed that maybe he had had a bad night, a cold or something of the sort, only a few of them had been at the parish the previous day. To know that Rev. Braun's life was in grave danger that he was dangling between life and death. It seemed apparent that the information had not been spread widely. It had been concealed from the rest of the parishioners and only those who were at the parish that morning knew what was happening and incidentally had not turned up for meditation that morning.

A week after Rev. Braun's death, he was buried as was willed by him in the parish cemetery. It was agreed that his family would be allowed to stay in the parsonage until when they finally left for home. This favour was accorded the family by the parish Board of Deacons. Newit had never felt empty as he did after Braun's death; he had come to consider Braun as his elder brother and a real friend. He contemplated on life's paradox, why would death always rob the world of the best, while those we wish dead live for as long as Methuselah. Life for Newit was moving from one calamity to the other, he finally concluded that had it been, life had a formula, many would live for eternity.

"Life continues," Newit said to himself as he realised that no amount of regret could turn back the hands of time. He however resolved that henceforth, he was going to be around the Braun's family for the close to one year they still intended to live in Cameon, at least that would be his own way of honouring and paying respect to his departed friend and mentor.

As the days went by, Newit finally decided to give in to the yearning that was building up within him, he gradually realized that Diane could not be shelved or discarded into the dustbin. What this woman did in his life still marvelled him, steal into his life and then impose herself and then proceed to taking his heart hostage. Had it been Emeline had stayed, he might never know that there could be better women in the world who were so hard and yet soft, strong and yet tender. That same day as the hot afternoon sun gradually transformed itself in a lame setting glow Newit convinced that he was responding to a call that could no longer be suppressed or denied then decided to make the long awaited phone call. As he dialled up Diane's house number, his heart sank and thudded as if it was going to explode like a landmine. He tried to take control of himself. He was dressed in an English made cotton sweatshirt, flavoured by the fragrance of his after-shave that could have won any lady's heart. After about what seemed like a century, he heard Diane's soft voice as she breathed in the mouthpiece that she had picked up and beautifully balanced in between her shoulder and her jaw.

"Hello!" he heard Diane's voice at the other end of the line. "Hello Diane, it's me."

Diane quickly recognised Newit's heavy voice.

to say. Diane's heart missed a beat as the glass she held almost came crashing on the floor, she fought with herself trying to reconcile what she had just heard with the hard but handsome sparsely wrinkled face that sat looking her straight in the eye. Their eyes met and Diane's world almost came to a standstill, she struggled for a smile, as life seemed to have been drained from her little dimpled jaws.

"You…you embarrass me, I…I never thought…." she did not finish what she was struggling to say, she had always looked forward to this day but she had almost lost hope and thought that Newit just wanted things the way they were.

"Yes Diane, I kind of expected that reaction from you but I'm serious, will you marry me?" Newit remained insistent but Diane did not feel like staying on any longer with this man, whom she loved so well and had wanted all her life, but couldn't now muster the courage to say so.

"I am not feeling so okay, Newit, I'll have to go, I need some rest, I'll reach back to you tomorrow." With those words, she was gone like the wind. Newit looked on perplexed cursing himself for having been so naïve. He tried and finished his drink, paid the bills and left, satisfied that at last, he had said it.

Early the next morning, Newit was woken up from bed by the persistent singing of the phone by his bedside.

"This is Newit, who's on the line?" Diane's shrill voice came thundering into Newit's ears; "Honey I want to tell you that I am sorry for what happened last evening, the problem is that I did not think you had me in such high esteem, I feel flattered."

The tension that had mounted on Newit's face gradually eased, everything came to a happy end as he heard Diane whisper into the mouthpiece again;

"I love you, I will marry you." Newit could not believe his ears, for he thought as Diane walked out on him last evening she had equally walked out of his life forever. How stupid he was, he concluded that he would never in his life understand what stuff women were made up of. They walk in today, tomorrow, they walk out, and the next day they walk in again. He whispered to himself "women" as Diane dropped the phone. He got up from bed, after having had a shave decided to have a warm shower for the morning was damned cold, unlike any before.

Mrs. Gemun had resumed work after the short sick leave she had. She looked pale though, gaunt and a bit older, but the usual smile and vivacity were still there.

"Sir, your breakfast is ready," she reminded Newit, who sat on a soft settee, lost in his own thoughts of his childhood days.

"Thank you, Stella." As he called out Mrs. Gemun's first name as if he was daydreaming. After he had his breakfast, he came and sat down on the same settee as he set his mind back to the past and reviewed his life as if he was watching it in a reel tape, step after step. He tried to remember what his father must have looked like. He did not get the chance of enjoying paternal love that some children of his childhood days had. The similarity struck him strongly as he realized that because of Emeline, his only son, his only blood Mandala his own progeny was deprived of fatherly love from him. This realization hit like a powerful hailstone, because it made him to come to terms with the fact that he was not or had never afforded his son, the paternal love, he had wished for before he ever got married to Emeline. He came to understand what his father was like from other people, he did not have that firsthand experience, he was so bitter because of the fact that unlike his father, who died when he was still a kid, he was still alive and had failed to raise up his son because of Emeline, whom he had so much trusted blindly. Had it been he had listened to his friends he wouldn't be in the mess in which he now found himself. He had almost fallen out with some of his friends, who told him that Emeline was seeing a certain white automobile salesman by name Jack Hank. He forced himself to forget this whole story but it wouldn't go away so easily. Memories of his childhood days were what he couldn't part with, they came whenever, even when he least wanted to be reminded of anything in his past. Newit always remembered what his mother looked like, though he couldn't give her any face, because when she passed away, he was only twelve and had just gotten into elementary school. He got into school thanks to a certain white missionary Rev. Grant who was a friend of his father's and whom his father had worked for as a house boy. His uncles had refused sending him to school, preferring that he got for himself something doing with his hands that could fetch him some money to take care of himself and his mother, both of whom were considered as burdens. The words of his paternal uncle Jifor, came to his mind with all vividness and pain as if it was just yesterday, that he was told those words.

"Newit you're now a big man, you can fend for yourself and that mother of yours, who killed her husband. I don't have money to waste on you, you better forget about going to school or you forget about me. Is that clear?"

"Y…es, yes, uncle but…" He did not know what else to say as his eyes were already flooded in a stream of tears. Though Jifor refused sending him to school, he still went to Rev. Grant in defiance of what he was told by his uncle. Rev. Grant was one of the first missionaries to have been to Nfui,

56

Newit's home village. He was a jovial man with a hot temper and spoke very little. He was well liked in Nfui.

Newit went to him he told him;

"I like to go to your school, pastor". Grant was very much excited by this little boy's ingenuity. Boys his age were interested in tending their father's goats while getting ready to assure parental responsibilities by age fifteen. Rev. Grant spoke English as if he did it through his nostrils.

"Yeah sonny, you wanna go to school? Now tell me do you like school?"

"Yes pastor I already have chalk." Rev Grant asked him to go home, help his mother do some chores, assuring him that he was going to think about what to do for him. He went home and told his mother what had transpired between him and Rev. Grant. His mother contrary to his expectations was very angry and had him well thrashed.

"You little devil, I know that you were going to bring me trouble in this house. Who sent you to say such thing to Pastor, I think you're going to stop going to doctrine if you think you can disgrace me and your father." Newit was very proud of his mother, though they wallowed in misery, she wouldn't just accept anything from whomever. So it was quite a task for Rev. Grant to convince her to allow Newit attend the St John Baptist Mission School Nfui. He was one of the youngest when he got to school for there were boys in his class as old as twenty. Newit happened to have been quite a brilliant boy and topped his class, so this made Rev. Grant take particular interest in his education. When Newit was leaving elementary school, his only regret was that his mother was not there to see him graduate, for she died just a few months after Newit got into school. Therefore, his uncle Jofor tried every manoeuvre to get him out of school to no avail. Newit still remembered what his uncle told him after his mother's death;

"You must leave that your white man's school now that your witch of a mother is dead or you join her." The reflection brought some hot tears to his eyes and he was amazed at how vulnerable he was to emotions, despite his age. He did report the matter to Rev Grant, who went to the village Chief, Afon, who out of shame for the presents that he was given by pastor such as woollen fabrics, strong gin, conceded to Grant's wishes to keep Newit.

The Afon said:

"Jofor you cannot keep this boy, because you cannot afford all these things this white man does." Jofor responded angrily:

"But…but Afon you know this child now belongs to me, so I can…not."

"Cannot what?" The Afon cut in, his decision was final, Newit was henceforth supposed to live with Rev. Grant.

Newit also remembered vividly how when he completed school, Jofor attempted to stop him from going to college in the south of the country, in one of the secondary schools of the Baptist Mission. One fine morning, he came to the mission yard dressed like a boxer and carrying with him a machete with which he threatened Rev. Grant. He burst into Grant's house with two persons who were also combat-ready, Jofor could not imagine himself seeing his good-for – nothing child who should have been working in his farms, go to this white man who was believed to be some ghost from some river in some far away land.

"Mr Whiteman, you better stay away from this boy or lose that your shell of a head now." he charged on with his pointed machete. Rev. Grant was really frightened as he

58

gestured with his hand for Newit to go. Jofin charged on and dragged the little boy by the shoulder as he cried out.;

"Leave me, leave me, I'm not going with you, leave me." But his cries were of no consequence as the two bloodthirsty looking men pulled him along as he kicked his little legs in the air and struggled to break free. It was due to the chief's timely intervention who upon receiving the news immediately summoned Jofor to his palace, who was threatened with banishment and charged a fine of ten goats if he did not release the boy within six hours, from the time of departure from the palace, he was to consider himself persona non grata in Nfui. That same day, Jofor shamefully surrendered the little boy back to Rev. Grant. About a week after the incident, Grant with the consent of the chief sent Newit down south to college.

Newit leaning back in his chair, reminiscent of his university days, remembered how he and his Ghanaian friend, Koffi met at Columbia University and were really pieces of curiosity to white students as they were chased round the campus to recount weird stories about Africa. Emeline was Sociology major and also from Cameon and it was but natural for them to grow to like each other and eventually got married. But their problems began the day Emeline said, she wanted to stay on in the States. Newit tried unsuccessfully to convince her to return with him to Cameon but to no avail and so things eventually degenerated between them, until one day, Emeline suggested divorce. Newit had felt as if all the intestines in his stomach were on a stampede, a deadpan expression had invaded his face and he clenched his fist in an apparent attempt to stay in control. What infuriated Newit the more was the fact that Emeline took advantage of the tender age of their son, Mandala who by then was still being suckled. She was given custody of their son exclusively until he was five. Newit couldn't wait even a year longer as he felt the increasing urge to go back home and serve his country. Hardly had Newit known that his own wife, Emeline was sleeping with Jack Hank an automobile salesman who lived some five blocks from their apartment. Newit now felt that all the years that he's been home in his own country were years of pain at the remembrance o f those old days. He often wondered whether it was even worth the pain to have come back, was his country worthy of his services or was he worthy enough to serve his country. He could not tell which was right. After about two hours of self-examination, incrimination and vindication, in a typical macho man act, he came to the realization that had it been, he were a bit fore-sighted, things wouldn't have gone the way they did in his life. He lashed out at himself in an indignant voice as if delivering a catch up lecture to himself in a voice huskier than usual;

"If you don't have use for your eyes, you had better given them to a blind person." If it wasn't true, then why could he not have seen the writing on the wall when he got married to Emeline?

6

As the plane took off from the J.K.F airport in New York, Emeline's heart missed a beat as she wondered what fate was reserved her back home. She and Mandala were among the one hundred and fifty passengers that boarded the Boeing 749 of Swissair, which was bound for Paris, from where Emeline and Mandala were to take a connecting flight to Banta. The chitchat in this big plane was in as many as six different languages. Emeline and Mandala were besides some French, Chinese, Dutch German and Spanish businesspersons as well as some tourists and students. Mandala kept on pestering her mother with a battery of questions; he looked younger than his almost twenty one year. He asked his mother in a dry undertone;

"Mum, what does Cameon look like? Is daddy still at NUC?"

His mother in a crisp voice, gave him a quick stare and said curtly, "I don't know. How do you expect me to know? Have I not all along been with you here in the States? How do you expect me to know?"

Mandala gave a nod as if he was being forced into submission.

Emeline in anguish fixed a grin as if to tell her son, "Don't you puck your little nose into matters that don't concern you. Why don't you just grow up then you will understand."

But there were no words that could materialise these thoughts. The realization came to her mind like a stray bullet, how she had all along been refusing her son, paternity, always giving him the impression that his father was a good-for-nothing bookworm whose mind had been eaten up by books. Emeline who was just three months away from her fifty-fifth birthday equally looked far more younger than her age, her beauty could still attract some hot lustful shots from the men that sat around her, the fragrance of the Eddie Bauer perfume she wore could have made the hardest of hearts soft and it was this weapon that Emeline carried about with much arrogance. She removed from her handbag a red band and bundled her tousled hair into it, this matched the small beautiful face that effectively defied age. It now dawned on Emeline that her two week long holidays back home was not going to be an easy one. The thought of encountering Newit haunted her, she wondered what his new wife looked like, was she more beautiful than she was? Emeline though divorced now with Jack still had a secret admiration for Newit if not love but if and only if, he had accorded her the love she so desperately needed when they just got married. Things wouldn't have gone the way they did. Though Emeline's aim of going home after twenty-eight years of living in the states was to visit her relations as well as to let his son have the opportunity to see what home looked like, she was also on a secret mission which was that of imposing herself on Newit and on whoever his new wife was. She had got the information from Jane her childhood and school days friend, who was a teacher in one of the public high schools in Banta. She was the one who kept her in touch with every bit of information and gossip concerning whoever or whatever. They did speak for two, three hours on the phone until; all the gossip there was in the whole world was finished. Her thoughts were disrupted by the soft voice of the hostess, who looked school girlish in her attire asked;

"Madame, que-je apporter pour vous?" Emeline felt blood leave her veins as the young blonde glared at her.

"Umh… le thé seulement" she fizzled out. The hostess continued…"et pour monsieur?"

"La meme chose," Emeline muttered with a wry smile. She hadn't realized that her son was deep asleep against her shoulder. She felt overwhelmed by some feeling of possession and wondered what her life would have been like had it been Mandala was with Newit.

When Emeline woke up from sleep she heard the soft but audible voice from the cockpit Mesdames ,messieurs, attachez vos ceintures, nous sommes a cinq minutes de Paris" Emeline suddenly felt ashamed when she realized that she had been the only one still sleeping. She looked heavy-eyed as she flashed her pale eyes on Mandala whose head was buried in the latest copy of Ebony Magazine. "Mandi," Emeline called out to Mandala as he was fondly called.

"Yes mum, had it been we had an accident, you would have died without you realizing what was going on?" Emeline felt as if Mandi's statement had pierced her heart and she retorted;

"You're the one who slept most, only that you got up earlier. Come on, any time from now we would be landing on French soil, doesn't it sound great to be in De Gaulle's country even if for a few minutes?"

Emeline's words were more of a statement than a question as she asked in apparent attempt to divert her son's attention from the magazine as she fastened her seat belt.

"It sure sounds great how I wish we could spend the night here". Mandi fizzled out and her mother was forced to give a loud mirthless laugh as they were soon engulfed in a tout silence as the plane's wheels soon screeched down the

Mandi who all along the drive had been quiet and felt most tired, he seemed to have been travelling for a month on end.

Jane finally muttered; "Here we are," as she pulled up in front of her house at Rue Braqueurs, a street that was renowned for the criminals it harboured. Emeline gave a limp gaze, rattling out;

"You have a nice place here, how I wish I had one, all the same I…" "But Daddy certainly has a place like this I guess" Mandi cut in, in a cheerful undertone like his father's. Those words kind of sent some shock waves down the spine of Jane, who had had safety forgotten about Newit for the moment deciding to play the pacificator as she blurted out;

"Yes Mandi, your father has a real nice place that you will certainly like when you meet him." She tried in a desperate attempt to keep things under control at least for now. Mandi's mother in a dismissive manner and in a voice that was tinged with anger ordered."

"Mandi you better stop that interrogation of yours and get those bags out of the hood" Mandi looking dazed, and automatically obeyed as if he was driven by some supernatural force.

It was a bright April morning and though it was the rainy season, the rains had fallen sparingly and Banta looked unusually and eerily dry because of the prolonged dry season. There was unbearable heat all over the place, people preferred to stay outdoors at least to have a gust of fresh air touch them if fresh air it was. There was suffocating heat especially in those households that could not afford fans. Though fans were a basic necessity, there were still many who considered it a luxury simply because they couldn't displace other items on their scale of preference for it. The sewers

66

were all stinking and the people who lived in most of the run-down neighbourhoods had already conditioned their nostrils to be stench proof. It was like a custom that once you took up residence in one of those neighbourhoods, you weren't to be told what to do or what to expect, you simply had to learn by observing what everybody was doing. Sewage from homes did no longer follow the sewage canals as most of them had been burst and so it was not uncommon to find shit and other unimaginables freely flowing down the streets into nearby streams that had been transformed into eternal sewage farms. There were some dogs in the neighbourhoods whose alimentary systems had undergone modification by virtues of them living in these neighbourhoods, they fed on these sewage deposits and grew healthier, if you saw a skinny dog then that dog hadn't learnt its lesson well. Also, one could mistake the neighbourhood rat moles for porcupines, these rat moles were most courageous, they cohabited with tenants of houses but refused to pay their own share of the rent, they were no longer afraid of humans since they had already been accepted as part of the family. People died like flies in these neighbourhoods from every conceivable illness, people no longer mourned the death of their loved ones for it was a relief to the families as one dead meant minus one mouth and most importantly a fund raising occasion for the family concerned, which under normal circumstances could not raise the vast sums of money that it did in these circumstances.

Crime was no problem any longer, it was a way of life. You had to commit one or the other crime in order to stay alive, it was like you join the bandwagon or you perish. Life was flushed out of people on a daily basis; indeed, nobody could claim to be safe any longer. The little or the nothing a man had was snatched from him by the children of his next

"Only one does sah, Abel". Stephane immediately felt ashamed and considered himself a failure to be telling a stranger that he was unable to send his children to school. Newit in a typical gentleman's style told Stephane with the badge of his company dangling from his chest pocket over his dark military pants that blended perfectly with the dust that had already enveloped them.

Newit declared to the consternation of both his wife and Stephane that he would as if in solidarity with the haves-not which Stephane represented sponsor all of his children to college. Stephen stood dazed and immediately went on his knees as if considering his benefactor for God and screamed;

"Let Allah be praised! Thank you, thank you, Sah."

Diane looked on dumbfounded as an embarrassed grin invaded her face, Newit told Stephane to stand up and to stop behaving like a child, but Stephane wouldn't for joy was suffocating him for such magnanimity.

Newit and Diane decided to withdraw indoors for it was already dark. It was already a week after Newit and Diane had been married, Diane had already moved into Newit's place to assume her domestic responsibilities as Newit's wife. They got married in a private ceremony that was blessed by Rev Ntubo, the new Parish pastor of the La Fontaine Baptist Church who replaced Rev. Braun. Diane felt now as if life was beginning anew for her, it was already some ten years since Diane was widowed. She was very enthusiastic about getting married especially at the beginning to marry Newit, there was one thing that gave her cold feet and explained her behaviour the day Newit proposed to her at the La Bonne Cuisiniere and that was the fact that she still doubted if her children, Ben, Frank and Joan all of whom were in France would be at ease with the fact that she was remarried. So she sought their consent and they to her chagrin were very happy that their mother could at last find joy after the untimely death of their father in that dreadful plane crash.

Diane decided to make supper, which consisted of roast fish, roasted on a grill, seasoned with ground spices, onion and pepper. This delicacy was known here as 'poisson braise' and was usually accompanied by hard cassava paste that was wrapped into bundles and commonly called 'baton'. Diane also bought some wine, to flush down this food. This food was a favourite of Newit's and this reminded him of the fact that any young man could be sure to win any young lady's heart by offering her this delicacy. He tried to remember last when he had eaten food that was prepared by his wife before he met Diane, and frightfully enough it was more than twenty years ago when things were still moving between him and Emeline.

That name Emeline, which he had tried all through those years to shelve but had found it impossible. He decided to tell Diane about Emeline as if that would make his burden lighter. He began;

"Dear, you know I've never liked to talk about Emeline, my ex-wife to you." Diane nodded in approval unable to understand what had prompted Newit to reopen that dreadful chapter of his as he had come to make her understand. She took a quick sip of her wine as if bracing up for a bloody confrontation.

"I know, you've never liked to talk of Emeline, so what about her now?"

"I kind of feel that Emeline closed my world as far as women are concerned, when she walked out on me for that salesman of hers, and until you stole into my life, I have never felt the way I do now." This was the part of Newit's past that

71

he had never told anybody about and so Diane was the first person to whom Newit confided this. He took another cup of the Spanish wine and became a little bit tipsy and felt like drinking his way through the wine-cellars. Diane looked on embarrassed as her eyelids dilated and she stared at Newit and became unnerved by his queer behaviour.

"Hey! you better stop drowning yourself in that wine, does your falling in love with me explain your getting drunk?" before she could finish her sentence, Newit was already was slumped on the dining table, Diane infuriated, got up from her seat and supported Newit on her shoulders as she led him into the bedroom. She cursed herself for having to go through these things again, after all it was part of her lot as a wife, indeed she was seized by some red-hot rage that she decided that the best thing to do now was to keep cool, it was the next day that Newit was to see the other side of her and learn never to take her for granted again.

It was already Emeline's second day in Banta, she could not bear the tropical heat that everyone else seemed to have accepted, willingly or unwillingly since there was no real alternative. Jane had already briefed her on Newit. She now possessed ample information concerning him and his new wife Diane and was now poised to confront him only if to prove to him that she was still the Emeline he got married to some many years ago. She had also learnt that Newit had been thrown out of his teaching job and was now a nobody; she wished that had served him right, she was to be accompanied by Jane, who knew where Newit lived as well as Mandala. She swore to herself that Newit wasn't going to claim any right over her son; she was just going to show him her son just for him to know that their son was now grown up and a senior at the University of California at Berkeley.

The doorbell rang twice before Diane went to the door to see who it was at the door this afternoon; they expected nobody apart from the refrigerator repairer who was to do some repair work with the refrigerator. She was dressed in a ribbed T-Neck Sweater over Timberland jean trousers and looked relaxed as she approached the door. When she opened the door, she was glued to the floor and she uttered in a whimpering voice;

"Can I help you ladies?" standing in front of her were two ladies who from their appearance seemed to be in their late forties and a young man dressed in a men's solid Twill shirt over light tan khaki pants perfectly matched by brown trekkers looking like some college sportsman. Jane was the one to speak first.

"Yes madam, we're looking for prof" as Newit was fondly called. Diane stepped by and opened the door wider for the trio to come in; she went on trying to sound friendly:

"Come right in and make yourselves comfortable," and hurried up the stairs, her heart playing a trick on her and beating faster that a stopwatch. Jane and Emeline as well as Mandala came in and settled down into three couches. The sitting room was adorned with two separate bookshelves of assorted books raging from the liberal arts to the hard-core sciences. Newit kept some of his books in his sitting room and the rest in his study that was the room next to his bedroom. Some of the books were offered him by his university professors and which he jealously kept and the rest were gotten by his sweat.

Newit suddenly appeared at the top of the staircase leading down to the sitting room, with a face as dry as a piece of paper with Diane by his side carrying a mutinous expression on her face. As he descended the stairs, Jane instinctively got up as if propelled by some mechanical force, Emeline sat still with a self-mocking grimace, she felt her throat go dry as if a lump had forced out air there. Mandi sat restlessly on the couch wondering whether this was a movie scene or reality. When Newit was some few paces from Jane, he as if struggling for breath stuttered;

"Is...is that my son?" pointing at Mandi. Both Jane and Emeline were flabbergasted and Jane managed to mutter lamely;

"Yes." Newit hesitantly strode across the rug to where Mandi sat and gestured to him to come into his waiting arms and Mandi responded with equal measure and fell into his father's arms as some hot tears ran down both of their eyes, Newit clung firmly to Mandi as Jane looked on dumbfounded and Emeline's mind went wild; she was seethed with jealousy. The mood was explosive and it was Diane's word that played the trick

"I, I guess this should be Mrs Hanks, nice meeting you," as she extended her hand to Emeline with a guarded expression in her eyes, Emeline hesitated but shook the hand. Diane equally shock hands with Jane who then sat down. Diane also shook hands with Mandi and uttered in a sardonic voice;

"You are a man now, Mandi, your father often talks about you." Mandala overwhelmed by the events that unrolled before him forced a smile as Newit patted him and said:

"I'm really, really glad to see you again my boy". He then turned first to Jane and greeted her and then to Emeline after some hesitation, drew her into his arms as Diane looked on, jealousy causing havoc within her. He then said in an indignant undertone, "thanks for bringing back my son." for his mind could not just visualise what to say to this woman who ruined his life but still had the guts to come into his matrimonial home, he only hoped it was nothing further than just a visit. Or better still, she was here to give him back his son, whom he so much missed. Emeline in a voice that was tinged with anger, bellowed,

"there is your son, I'm here just for a short visit and I'll be going to the village after tomorrow to greet my mother and we'll be leaving in two weeks, so don't think that Mandi will stay back with you, I'm taking him back with me."

No mum, I'll stay, Mandala cut in to Emeline's chagrin who immediately shouted at him; "stop that free-mouthing of yours, you're going back with me, I shouldn't have brought you in the first place. Mandi gritted his teeth in apparent defeat, for he knew when his mother was serious. Newit took Emeline's word in a relaxed manner, for he equally understood who Emeline was as he tried to change the topic by introducing Diane.

"This is my wife Diane, Diane meet my ex-wife Emeline." Both ladies hesitated then as if out of compulsion shook hands again while casting each other hot glances. Diane equally shook hands again with Jane as well as with Mandi.

Jane who all along had been in the background for all this time decided to make her presence felt by saying, "They are staying with me at my place, you should feel free anytime, you choose to see them."

"Thank you, Jane," Newit uttered indignantly believing that Emeline had been sufficiently furnished with information concerning him by Jane for she was very flippant.

Diane in an apparent attempt to sound diplomatic asked her guests, "What can I offer you, Baron de valls, Vinosol or you would like beer or soft drinks?"

"Oh! No, we have to get going, I'm sorry Mrs. Lobe, we must get going now," Jane snapped. They were already up but Mandi was still seated as if he did not want to go any longer.

"What are you still doing there or you want to stay here? Get up, let's go." Mandi lazily got up and his father stood staring at him eye to eye and was really pleased to see that his son was now a man.

He only knew that his son was in university. He held his hands in his and asked:, "What do read in university and what year are you?"

"Biology and I'm a senior at Berkeley." Newit was mad with joy to learn that his son was already a senior at and attending the prestigious University of California.

"You want to do medicine I guess?" He probed further.

"Yes, dad, but mum says I don't have the brains." His mother shot a hot glance at him as he continued implacably,

"Dad, I'm not gonna let you down."

Newit felt elated and said thoughtfully, "Son, I know you're going to make it just like your father." He was embarrassed by the resemblance his son had with him. Though he was of a short build, he could make a good athlete just like he did in his own school days. Newit went on, "What sport do you do?"

"Basketball," Mandi responded immediately.

"I hope you're doing pretty well in it, I hope you beat the Jordans. As for me, I used to play soccer though my niche was in track and field, regrettably I didn't go far with it."

Mandala's mother shrugged her shoulders and commanded:

"Hey you there, don't get on my nerves, you think we're gonna stay here?' Can't you get that into skull?"

She turned to Diane,

"We have get going but before I forget, I wish you the best in your matrimonial home, I hope you make him what I didn't succeed to, hope you understand, uhm!"

Diane stood rooted to the ground as if caught by some spell. Newit let go of his son's hands and led him to the door. When they were already outside, a few and just metres away from Jane's Peugeot 405 car, the couple bid their guests goodbye. Mandi's eyes went already wet with tears as he got into the passenger seat. Emeline was the last to get in and sat alone at the back seat of the car. After having told Newit with a wry smile she hoped he was a happy man now that he was remarried to a younger more beautiful lady, whom she found difficult to come to terms with Jane waved at both Newit and Diane and reversed the car out of the yard as Stephane flung wide open the gate. When the car was out of sight, Diane came and leant an elbow on Newit's shoulder while supporting her body with the other hand at her waist and whispered into Newit's ears with a mocking grin on her face;

"Is that the woman you married?" Newit understood the message without further explanations and was led indoors by Diane, hands clasped into his. He didn't utter a word, his mind was going through an inferno and he heard his inner self warm him; "she's not through with you yet." But Newit was glad for at least one thing, he had seen his long lost son again after a very long time, he gave a sigh of relief and remarked to Diane's hearing:

When fate pinches you on one jaw, it soothes you on the other. As for Diane, she had come to understand just in a single day what stuff, Newit's ex-wife was made of, she had to tow the line, but she told herself that Emeline should make no mistake for she would do whatever it takes to remain happily married, Emeline shouldn't fool herself that she was capable of wrecking her home.

7

The country was caught by a very high fever, a fever that surpassed all medication, the country was very very sick, so it was rumoured in the streets, every beer parlour, slum, bus, cab and home. It was not uncommon to find groups of people gathered around street corners speaking in muted voices. There was tension that had gradually built up during the years, and had reached bursting point. One could find peasants, the uniformed officers, the business barons shouting to whoever wanted to listen that "enough is enough". It was rumoured that the uniformed officers were disgruntled with the way things were run and were now themselves prepared to take over. The opposition had literally been silenced, the firebrands of the opposition like Garba Mansa had been bought over and officially, there was an opposition, but the party in government had become supreme, indeed even the president's sneeze was law. There was fear, fear of the unknown, everybody had the premonition that something dangerous was about to happen but nobody could say for sure what.

People consulted the witch doctors, astrologers and those who still went to church, offered their lives in prayers in order to save themselves and the nation from the ordeal that was overhead that nobody could predict. But one thing was for sure that the nation was in grave danger. Was it that God was angry with the country? How could he, when there were still some good grains, among the bad ones? Wasn't it said that God was all-forgiving? Then all was not lost though neither the priest not the marabout could say for sure.

People were dying like flies, flies were at least better, because they did not bother about hospitals, life had come to mean so little, life was no longer a right but a favour you could jolly well take away your own life or let someone do it for you if you couldn't do it on your own. There were people who were living corpses, hanging on, hoping that things might get better one day, so one was told that no matter what, never give up hope. There were so many means of dying, you could decide to work yourself to death, and when you couldn't, a mosquito bite could help you do it. Wasn't it said that there was a heaven where there is milk and honey for all? Why not kill those who seemed to be living in permanent pain so that they could have an early enjoyment of that heaven?

One had to become a clergyman in order to stay alive, the church it seemed was the winning bet, no doubt, and everybody was either becoming a priest or pastor. Churches sprung up like mushrooms. Oh yes, didn't Jesus, an individual found a whole church to which over one fifth of the world belonged, wasn't that a signal to whoever could see that everybody should become his co-worker? Didn't he say, he did not come to efface the teachings of Moses but to complement them? So somebody else could compliment his work and so the number of the men of God kept increasing.

"Who said, who said…..? Is the question, anybody could ask hadn't others, then why shouldn't I?" Foulabe Yosa couldn't understand why things were happening the way they did. Yosa was a young man in his late twenties, heavily bearded, and resembled some Afghan warrior, he had abandoned university studies in second year at NUC, where he was doing double honours in philosophy and African studies. When asked why he left school, Yosa said he couldn't stand the sight of those brainwashed western trained professors telling him what he wasn't.

"Do you know what I think?, I'm going to lead a revolution in this country, it doesn't matter whether I get killed, and should I die, I would have fulfilled my own part of the divine commission from Allah." Yosa would say as if controlled by some spirit. He breathed heavily as he shot wild hungry, revengeful glances at Newit, who had sat quietly listening as if bound by a spell. Newit felt sympathy for this young man, who like thousands was ready to give up their lives for a cause that was difficult. Newit in a soft compassionate fatherly voice tried to sound realistic;

"Look here, Yosa, don't think that I don't understand how you feel, indeed I do, we are in the same camp, but I want you to be cautious, be slow to anger, think well, plan before you act, I know what I'm talking about" It was Newit's turn to feel his own pain for what he had gone through in the hands of those who governed. It was at this point that it dawned on him that he shared so much with this young man, he came to know when he was dispensing a course on African political thought to students in the Department of African Studies. Yosa was outspoken, challenging and interesting. He had challenged Newit as to why African intellectuals couldn't develop their own political ideologies which could compete with those of the western world. Newit was dumbfounded and managed to utter something that did not sound convincing to the young man and so he decided to have a further discussion with him after class. He came to like Yosa whom he found to be very ingenious and courageous. But he was sad when he learnt that Yosa had left school to join the military, where he hoped to transform his revolutionary ideals into reality. According to

Yosa, there was only one way to salvage the situation in the country and that was through the barrel of the gun, though he was just a warrant army officer.

Although Newit was in favour of change, he did not quite buy the idea of a coup because he reasoned that things had not yet gone bad to that level. All he knew was that someday, things were going to get better, and how they were going to he did not know. Yosa after listening to Newit, who to him sounded complacent with those who governed in a faltering voice burst out,

"Thank you sir, all the same but what I have to do, just nobody can stop me. I am going to ...." He did not finish what he was about to say as Newit cut in, in silky persistence while Yosa stared on woodenly.

"Look here, Yosa, change will come someday, so we don't have to precipitate it, do you see the point I'm trying to make?" Yosa wasn't convinced at all but knew in his mind that if there was one person for him to rely on for advice on God's earth, it was Newit.

"Thank you sir, I think I have to get going, I have to catch up with my colleagues at the barracks but I promise to keep in touch with you."

"Well, you're welcome any time". Newit muttered as Yosa stood up to his full six feet twenty, rapidly emptied his cup of beer, put on his beret and gave Newit a typical military hand cut. He heard his footsteps clatter on the steps of the threshold outside and from that moment he knew Yosa might never come back so he was warned by his premonition that never failed him.

The next day as early as 3:00 am, Newit woke up from bed, panting, his heart was beating in a most unusual manner he was barely gasping for air, fear seized him, he was not himself, he had never felt so before, he immediately knew that things were not fine but couldn't say what wasn't. He got up from bed, wrapped up in a shawl collar robe and headed for the kitchen to find something to calm down his anxiety with. After having gulped down a glass of milk, he felt as if a heavy load had been removed from his head. When he got back to the room, Diane was leaning on one shoulder on the bed as she threw a wild glance at her husband as if that was the first time to see him. She had never seen Newit as nervous as he was this morning. She immediately knew that there was something wrong.

"Honey, what's the problem, you're not sleeping, and it's still five past three." Her eyes then went to the alarm clock by the bedside cupboard to confirm what she had just said.

"I'm, I'm having some light headache but everything will be fine." Newit tried to sound reassuring. He drew himself back to bed feeling as if his legs would give way below. When he climbed into bed, Diane rolled herself closer to him as she sent one hand into Newit's robe and pleasurably caressed his chest hair. When she realised that her trick had succeeded, she murmured,

"Honey, can you now tell me the problem; I also think you married me for that." Newit took a deep heave, sprawled on the bed with his head resting in between his hands. He said thoughtfully,

"I have this feeling that something's wrong in this country but I can't say what."

"You don't have to bother yourself about what you can't see, it's no use, o.k., now go back to sleep, will you?" Diane seemed to have given a command that needed instant obedience. Newit obeyed without question and was lulled into sleep by the light sensuous caress of Diane's hands on his chest that did his body some good.

It was a cold chilly morning in Banta, most households were already up to begin the daily routing of life, going through the chores, making breakfast if there was any then hurrying off to line up the taxi queues to go to work if you could be counted among the privileged. The birds were still chirping from tree top to tree top as if in solidarity against the harsh weather, which had hindered them from going out for their own daily bread. The rainy season in Banta though it usually came as a relief to many, was also a nuisance. With the rains very much around, one had to procure a pair of rain boots if you wanted to look standard, but many were those who opted for rubber sandals that were commonly known as "changshoes". Few were those who could lay any claim to an umbrella, it was a luxury that everybody needed but which few had. There were those to whom storms meant nothing for they had conveniently forgotten about the existence of raincoats and umbrellas, their bodies were already used to hardship for want of an alternative, some even boasted of being rainproof.

Yes, the morning was unlike many, for even the petty traders who included peddlers and market women commonly known as 'buyam–sellams' were afraid to go out for the only thing, they could do if they must stay alive. The peddlers who were popularly called "attaquants" for their ingenuity to convince the hardest of hearts that the wares they were exhibiting on their bodies hanging round their heads and their hands were the best available in the market. They could brave all odds and could go any length to sell their wares. Even this seemingly absent but ever present force had refused to go out into this cold, unwelcoming morning that was not even the match of others they had encountered before.

This morning was different, there were no lights, they had gone out at about 4:30 am, most people who afforded waking up that early for various reasons were not surprised. The National Electricity Corporation (NEC) was notorious for all sorts of cuts, some that lasted for as long as a week and whose frequency was no news. Those who had electrical appliances had developed mechanisms to counter or reduce the impact of these blackouts. Yet, one had to pay bills, even when you had no electrical appliances; you could pay a bill as high as one who had a cold store. One had to always have a candle beside a reading lamp, so that you could immediately switch to the other source of light without delay and continue whatever it was that you were reading so this morning was just one of such mornings that Bantaits were used to but with a difference.

"What a morning" one child exclaimed unable to go to school early. For many children school was where to go and hide, far away from shouting bored parents, whose authority it seemed could only be exercised over their own progeny. In school, one could safely hide one's hunger from the knowledge of the others, only one's close friends could know. A crust of stale bread was a luxury. Yet you had to give the impression that you had had a breakfast of eggs and milk or perish. Though, the contours on one's face and one's crankiness could betray their malnutrition, you had to give a mirthful smile to the world that you were fine. The morning wasn't the one to go out, the storm was over, but there was still reluctance all over, for people to go into the rough world and do what destiny had decreed for them.

Newit was in the habit of always keeping some spare batteries in his bedside cupboard just in case the electricity people in their solo act cut the lights. He wasn't wrong today, he contended himself that he had always judged correctly. He had a small world receiver that would soon be celebrating its tenth anniversary of faithful service. After having loaded the receiver with the new batteries, he felt some satisfaction as he sat on the edge of the mahogany made bed to tune to the Cameon National Radio Corporation (CNRC) for what they had as news which was usually a repeat of either the RFI, BBC or the VOA as far as foreign news was concerned, some people contemptuously referred to CNRC as the praise singer of the government. Newit was interested in getting the analysis of the previous day's cabinet reshuffle at least the pro-government opinion. When the frequency indicator landed on 88.8 MHZ, only a hiss could be heard, an indication that the transmission lines were off. He made some frantic attempts at other private radio stations but all he could get was religious music. That increased his anxiety; there had never been such a situation as before. Diane saw him fumbling and asked if he was fighting with the radio receiver. He remained quiet in apparent frustration at his fruitless search. Wild ideas went through his mind as he changed band after band, finally trying VOA. His mind began to play a funny game on him, he wondered whether the president was dead or something like that had happened.

"No!" he exclaimed to himself as his inner self told him, "don't be foolish, you can never understand," when he finally got the VOA, a low shrill female voice came through with the lone headline of the six thirty news.

"Good morning and welcome to this half hour of news with the VOA. We have one lone breaking story in our news this morning; there has been a failed military coup in Cameon at about 4:00 am this morning. It is reported that the vice president as his bodyguard and six other top government officials were killed in the coup led by junior army officers. For details, we call on our reporter in Banta, Mary Aldridge who is standing by."

Newit immediately turned off the radio and threw it on the bedside cupboard fuming, to Diane's consternation, who up to now was still curled up in her blanket.

"What's the matter Honey." Diane managed to ask, she had never seen Newit in such a mood, his head was propped in between his hands and knees and he looked a horribly pathetic sight. He managed to gather himself together and shuttered in a most lame voice,

"There, there's been, a, a coup this morning." Life left Diane lovely eyes, she unwrapped herself and came to Newit's side stretched one arm round his shoulder and with a blank gaze on her face queried in a voice tinged with cynicism;

"Are you sure? Anyway, is that enough reason to look as if someone is dead? Um... now I understand why you didn't sleep at night." Newit did not utter any further word. He made a frantic effort to look fine but Diane knew that things were far from that.

A few minutes later, they had both breakfast of omelette with fried potato chips and were still at the dining table chit-chatting when the door bell rang, non-stop, they both cast hot glances at each other wondering what lunatic there was at the door this morning. Newit now dressed in a white nylon T-shirt over beach like multicoloured shorts opened the door expecting to see some mad person, but to his utmost surprise, he saw a soldier, a friend of Yosa's called Phillipe. He asked, anger still burning within him in a flat voice;

"Can I help you?"

"Yes sir, I am Phillipe Yosa's friend, I just felt I should pass round and inform you of his death."

"What? Is this some joke?" Newit crackled.

"No sir, actually Yosa was executed about an hour ago at the 'camp militaire' alongside nine others, for having staged a coup against the president."

Newit's pupils dilated further and he beckoned the young officer to come inside, who politely turned down the offer with the excuse that he was late for work. Newit was still transfixed by the door side as Diane who had already left the dining table strode her way in the direction of the two men to see what the soldier looked like.

"So, where is the corpse?" Newit splattered out. Phillipe had a dead pan expression on his face and immediately offered regrets as if he was before a military tribunal trying to plead for his life.

"The bodies were buried without anyone seeing them in a mass grave at the La foret Municipale , I'm sorry sir". Newit felt some cold shivers go down the length of his spine and Diane looked away in disgust for what she had first heard. Newit heard himself asking;

"When will all these ever end? Oh God!" at the embarrassment of both Diane and Phillipe who said,

"I didn't quite get you." Newit immediately excused himself that he had said nothing. The young soldier was already gone in a typical military style leaving Newit to the torture of his thoughts before he say goodbye in return.

It was still drizzling outside now, but still, there were very few people in the streets, a few had heard about the coup but the majority up to now were still ignorant of it. Newit warily followed Diane back into the sitting room frustrated by the fact that Yosa and his colleagues were executed without any judgement.

"This is Africa," he was immediately reminded by Diane, before he could go any further into thoughts that didn't go beyond that.

Newit's day was already spoilt by the bad news he got from Phillipe, Yosa's friend. He wondered why life had to be full of misfortunes. Reality suddenly hit him that he could waste his whole life trying to understand but would never understand. He also agreed with those who said 'if you can't beat'em then join'em'. But that was good advice for the weak not for someone like him, what should have applied for him was 'if you can't beat'em, then spit at'em.' But Newit seriously doubted how one could outsmart the system, which he fondly referred to as the vicious circle. How with little effort people could be made to disappear without a trace. How could one fight a void, when you couldn't even determine its nature? No, it wasn't worth the pain nor the brains to even contemplate fighting a life, destiny said is yours. Wasn't it also true, that fate imposes and man re-imposes himself? If it wasn't true, then man would always perish under the weight of an unjust fate, to which everything and everybody whatsoever and whosoever was a potential victim. Man had to fight back, if not at least, react, that was one of the reasons why man was endowed with the brain and the forearm.

Yes, life's journey was no easy one, but one needn't be chicken-hearted for when you became chicken-hearted, you had no place on this earth, it should have been better if you were born directly into heaven, to enjoy the eternal bliss. If you must live in this life you had two options either to beat life or perish. Newit wondered which of the two was true to him, his experience was a melange. Thank God, he still had Diane by his side to give him the support; he so badly needed at times like these. He couldn't say for sure what his life could've been like without this woman by his side. May be, he should've been dead or something of the sort.

Mrs Gemun had for sometime witnessed some changes in her role in the house now things were a little bit different. She had been everything to Newit when he was still single but now that he was married, a new chart had been mapped out for her. She wasn't so regular now at work, she had been sent on what she fondly called 'retraite anticipe' though she retained her full pay, this was simply a strategy by Diane to have enough time with her husband, with nobody around to disturb the feeling between them. Her role was now reduced as her role as cook was fully assumed by Diane who felt that she had to take full charge of what her husband ate and not somebody else. Mrs. Gemun's work ended at midday rather than 6:00 pm as was the case before. Mrs. Gemun was quite excited by the new order of things, as this gave her enough time to take care of her grandchildren who lived with her. Also the fact that she now worked for only three days a week, gave her ample time to go to her farm, which was second nature to her, unlike before when she had to beg for permission from Newit, although it was never denied.

8

Two days after the failed coup, two plain-clothes police officers came to Newit's place when he had gone out visiting. On leaving, he left a message with Mrs. Gemun that whenever anybody comes looking for him, she should tell the person that he and Diane had gone to Ganta's place who was sick and had just been discharged from hospital, so when Police Inspectors Jean Pierre Ntoa and Louis Ntep came to his place this morning on an investigation into the coup, precisely with instructions from the Bureau des Enquetes Criminelles to incriminate him, they were disappointed when they met instead a plump old lady.

When Mrs Gemun opened the door, she was startled and started in a faint voice, "Are you looking for somebody or something?"

"Oui. Madame, nous recherchons le Professeur Newit, est-il à la maison?" Jean Pierre Ntoa retorted in the only language he could ostentatiously lay claim to apart from his mother tongue. "Pardon monsieur, je vous comprends, mais le Prof. n'est pas à la maison."

Jean Pierre cast furtive glances at his colleague Louis Ntep who till now had remained silent. Louis uttered :

"Tu vois ce que je t'avais dire, il nous fuit, mais il ne va pas réussir." Jean Pierre nodded in agreement, fear seized Mrs. Gemun as she stood before these savage-looking men both dressed in French Tergal jackets, that seemed to be the unofficial uniform of the 'Enqueteurs Criminelles'. Before Mrs. Gemun could say, "vous ne laissez pas un message?" The two criminal investigators were already past the flower hedge, all Mrs. Gemun could do, was look in amazement at these two mad men, who were bold enough to just burst into somebody's home, ask questions and just leave without even saying who they were. Mrs. Gemun heard herself cursing 'thieves' but that was all she could do.

Immediately after the executions of Yosa and his colleagues, Newit and a couple of other persons, some of whom were already under police custody were suspected to have been behind the aborted coup by the junior military officers. The minister of Defense as well as some generals, colonels and the head of the presidential security had been arrested and it was believed within the governmental circle that some intellectuals such as Newit and some Cameonese in exile were also involved. But no direct link could be established. The President fondly called Chef knew that he could not just arrest Newit like that, given the fact that he was not just anybody. The memory of what his arrest did during the post electoral violence was still fresh. They did not want to severe relations with both donor countries and institutions and the human rights organizations were also on the watch. This meant that they had to be cautious and implicate Newit in a way that was beyond reproach.

The assignment that Jean Pierre Ntoa and Louis Ntep had was to establish a link between Yosa's visit to Newit, a few days to the failed coup with the coup's eventual execution. Newit immediately after his release was under police surveillance without his knowing, and so that evening that Yosa came to his place, the two security men were around and knew when Yosa went into his place and the time of his departure. The government was aware of the fact that Newit had had important connections abroad, and this could prove to be the much needed clue to his activities outside the country that were believed to be to the government's disadvantage. Now was the golden opportunity to teach Newit and others like him a lesson they would never forget till the day they embrace their miserable deaths. They had to be taught that you shouldn't look beyond your nose, that you shouldn't poke your nose into places that did not concern you. People like Newit had to be gotten rid of and as fast as possible without leaving any trace.

It had been about two weeks now, since Ganta had fallen ill, it was diagnosed at the 'Hopital classique de Banta' that he had renal failure and that one of his kidneys had to be removed and replaced, else he would die. In the meantime, while a volunteer was awaited, Ganta had been discharged temporarily after a round of chemotherapy. Diane was shocked when she saw the once lively Ganta looking so pale, she doubted if Ganta was going to survive, but earnestly wished that he did. Newit was as composed as ever, he had experienced such situations a thousand times before and had learnt by habit to keep calm. Ganta looked dull-eyed as he managed a smile towards his long time friend and mentor, Newit, who together with his wife Diane were ushered into Ganta's living room by his German wife known as Sonia whom he met when they were both graduate students back in the States. Sonia looked disturbed and older than she really was and could be mistaken for someone in her sixties; she had developed an eating disorder as a result of her worry over her husband's illness.

Ganta who was sprawled out on a couch asked Newit who was settling down on a nearby leather sofa, while Diane sat on a long settee by the window.

"Do you think I'll make it? Sonia tells me that I will but I doubt. I, I may die."

Newit didn't waste any time,

"No you ain't going to die; besides how do you feel?" Newit tried to dissuade Ganta from negative feelings and to make both him and Sonia to feel that all was not yet lost. And that is exactly what he and Diane succeeded to do, Sonia felt relieved and quite relaxed for the first time in two weeks with the visit of Newit and Diane also acknowledge the face that treatment was more of a psychological matter. That it's ones predisposition towards illness and their perception of their chances of survival that determine survival. When Newit and Diane left the Gantas, they were quite a different people from what they were prior to their visit.

Newit and Diane arrived home that evening at a little bit past seven. As Newit pulled the car to a stop in the car park, they were both surprised that lights were coming out from the windows, an indication that there was someone in the house. Diane's heartbeat increased as they climbed the steps, up the porch to the main door. Diane pressed her thumb to the doorbell button with all force that she could muster while Newit stood by watching. Mrs. Gemun immediately rushed to the door and flung it open as Newit and Diane filed past her into the sitting room. Mrs. Gemun did not wait for Diane and her husband to settle down before spluttering out in a faltering voice;

"Some two men were here this morning, to see, you sir, but refused to leave any message or their names." Newit did not look disturbed but Diane suddenly asked again for the second time,

"Mrs. Gemun, are you sure of what you're saying? Why didn't they stay?"

Stella, thank you". Newit couldn't wait any longer for Mrs. Gemun to undergo Diane's interrogation a second time.

"I think I'll have to go now, that's what made me to stay to now, to tell you myself. Good night."

"Stella, my regards to your grandchildren." Newit drawled behind her. Mrs. Gemun approached the door, suddenly turned round and stammered;

"Your supper's on the dining table I thought since you would be coming in late, I should prepare something." With those words, she was already gone past the door into the hot evening. Newit remarked 'Smart lady' as Diane looked on in bemusement. "If it wasn't for that lady, I should've been dead by now." Diane was stuck, she did not know what to say for her reason for removing Mrs. Gemun's other role as cook was to assume full responsibility over her husband's culinary needs Though she felt embarrassed, she was really hungry, they had both taken lunch together but that was about five hours ago. Newit immediately declared in an off-hand manner; "I'm dying of hunger, you're invited to join."

Diane as if under compulsion followed Newit into the dining room without a word.

Three days after the plain clothes police officers came to Newit's place, they were more prudent this time around in order to meet him at home, interrogate him and search his home. So when Newit was called out from his warm bed and informed by Diane that Inspectors Ntoa and Ntep were in the sitting room waiting for him, he wasn't surprised, because of the description, they were given by Mrs. Gemun, the other day they paid a visit to Ganta's. Newit who was dressed in check pyjamas growled:

"Yes Sirs, what I can do for you?" the taller and skinnier of the two men, who seemed to be in his mid forties and who dwarfed his companion he was conspicuously potbellied. He bellowed out;

9

The two security officers never returned as they promised, Newit was at a loss to explain why they didn't. How on earth could he be charged with arms possession, who was behind all these happenings? Who was he that was out to see his downfall? Wasn't the invasion by the security against his home a signal that someone was out to settle scores? But as far as he was concerned, he had not wronged anybody, had never even thought of such. He was quite anxious if someone could tell him, who and why that person was behind him, he would be the happiest man on earth.

It suddenly dawned on Newit that he hadn't paid his only friend, Ganta any visit for more than two weeks. He was worried about what his condition was now, that made him to feel a bit guilty. He decided that today he was going to pay him a visit. He wasn't sure whether Diane would accept to accompany him but all the same, he was going to try to persuade her in case she resisted. Diane was in the kitchen this morning in the company of her long time friend Margaret. They were chattering at the top of their voices, Mrs. Gemun was also in their company.

"You know, I always believed that you would make a good lawyer one day, Maggie." Diane said as she sliced some cabbages on a wooden chop board, Mrs Gemun was with the blender, trying to grind some spices.

"Hmh, what if I didn't, would you have forgiven me for failing?" Margaret retorted as a broad grin swept her childlike face, she sipped her wine with one hand and with the other adjusted the ribbon that delicately bundled her neat hair. She was seated by a small dining table that was meant for three which Newit liked so well, it often reminded him of his early days with Emeline, when Mandi was still a kid.

The conversation between the ladies continued for some two hours, Newit was still sprawled out relaxed on a couch trying to look at some of his PhD research papers. He was amazed by what time could do. It could certainly change everything in a twinkle of an eye. He now looked at his doctoral thesis from a different perspective, had it been he were a doctoral student now, he would have reasoned more maturely. From his position in the sitting room, he could eavesdrop the conversation of the three ladies in the kitchen. Before he could realize it, he was already fast asleep on the couch, with the papers clutched to his chest by one hand.

"You know, I don't always understand what pushed me into the legal field. I can bet you that the profession is not that enviable as people always think. You always have some bored old judges asking you to repeat each thing that you say. In order to make small money, one has to shout out one's lungs."

"Um, then I suggest you take some honey, that will keep your voice intact, that's what I always did when I was still in that damned classroom with the sleepy hungry children looking at me, and having to always fight with the chalk dust." Diane tried to comfort her friend, who was a virtual workaholic. Mrs. Gemun who was now at the sink, washing her hands queried:

"Why're you girls always into something that you don't like? You see I'd rather stay at home. I'll be back before you both know it." Diane had come to realize that without Mrs. Gemun she wouldn't succeed, she had come to mean

104

everything to her now, not just as a maid but a friend and a confidant. She was always marveled by Mrs. Gemun's frankness. She was struck by what Mrs. Gemun had just said. It was quite true that she had gotten into the teaching profession without liking it and that explains why she was in it for just over two years.

But those few years had been of paramount importance in her life, it was in that her cubicle of a classroom that she met Robert Nwato the school's contractor and purveyor who immediately fell in love with the young lady, fresh from high school and they eventually got married the next year. Diane often regretted why she left the teaching field.

Immediately after her marriage, she became the manager of Ladox Enterprise Ltd. She had a first child Stephanie when she was only twenty-two and Stepahanie was followed by John Paul and lastly by Tonye. Diane immediately assumed the ownership of all of Robert's businesses as was stated by his will when he died in a ghastly motor accident while rushing through the crowded streets of Banta to catch up a flight for a business trip to South Africa. When Diane reflected on her past, she felt like weeping.

After Robert's death, Diane lived for seven years without having anything to do with any man until when she met Newit three years ago. She had also transferred the management of all the business enterprise to his second child John Paul now twenty-seven who was now based in Paris together with his other siblings. She only came in from time to time to chip in a word or two of advice but tried as much as possible not to interfere with management.

Margaret was a distant cousin of Robert's and had come to be the only person in Robert's family that Diane was at ease with. She was the only one who stood by her when

Robert died; she also helped Diane to inherit Robert's property to the total opposition of the rest of Robert's family. She also helped her with the legal procedure. So Diane had grown to love her very much, but of late, their relationship had lost the steam of the early days because Margaret was an extremely busy person, had managed to keep in touch at least by phone.

After the four of them had lunch together, that is, Newit and the three ladies, Mrs. Gemun, Diane and Magaret, Margaret immediately rose up from the dining table, stretched out her arms and looking schoolgirlish in her Afritude attire drawled out:

"Whao! Quite full, you know I haven't really had time to eat something like this, now for weeks."

"And don't you think, you're on your way to self-destruction?" Newit blared struggling to make his point heard with his mouth full.

"I think I'll have to do something about that, Julie always blames me that she always has to eat out of cans." She gave a mirthful laugh. After lunch she walked out of the dining room with Diane who had joined her while Newit and Mrs. Gemun continued munching. Diane accompanied Margaret to a nearby garage on foot where she left her Renault car for the exhaust pipe to be checked; it seemed to have burst and was puffing out a hell of smoke.

By the time both ladies arrived the Garage Moderne de Petit Jean, the car was ready, she took the car keys from the middle aged mechanic got into it and throttled till she was satisfied with the man's work. She drew out a ten thousand francs note from her purse, gave it to the man as he bowed before receiving it like someone receiving communion. Both

Diane and Margaret chatted for a while; Margaret suddenly looked up her watch and screamed:

"Oh, My God, I must get going it's ready past two as she hugged Diane and then got into the car, fastened her seat belt and reversed the car out onto the potholed dilapidated tarred street. "Extend my love to Julie, I'll call round next week."

"Thank you Diane for everything, the food especially... till next week then, bye."

"Bye Maggie, take care." Diane waved as she continued standing and watched her friend's car disappear down the La Fontaine Street.

Later that day, in the evening, Newit and Diane paid Ganta a visit, who had improved substantially and was now able to walk about the house unaided. They were quite impressed and were also very glad to realize that life had returned to Sonia's face. She was no more the sad mask that she was the other day, when they had visited; she was now livelier and grateful to Diane for having comforted her throughout these very trying moments.

The papers carried the incident that happened at Newit's home in detail. The 'Clarion' in its caption; "Professor Newit again assaulted", treated the matter with such interest that surprised Newit. According to the Clarion, the government in its age-old struggle with the university don was out to eliminate him because he constituted such a formidable threat to its machiavellistic machinations to stay in power for eternity. The paper further intimated that the government had implicated Newit with the coup in order to justify his elimination and in order to achieve its aim; he was framed up together with some exiles to be the brains behind the coup, and accused to have been illegally importing arms.

which rested on his thighs and a drop of tear left his right check and landed on the carpet. He reflected over and over again on every single word of the better until it was well digested.

Yes, he now felt like a father, the pride of the father of the prodigal son overwhelmed him. But he immediately cautioned himself that his son wasn't any prodigal son but just one who had been taken away from him for too long. Now was the time to show his son that he had a father and one he should be proud of.

He took up the December edition of Newsweek opened the first page but wasn't able to gather himself together to read even a single line, he was still trembling with excitement like an innocent child abandoned in the bush that is crying for joy at the sight of his parents at the other end of the bush coming for him. He threw the magazine on the table and leant back on his seat, picked up the remote control and put on the T.V. again, but was swept away into sleep as he lay on his back on the settee. The television noised on but nobody was there to savour its images, except the cat that was safely hidden under the central table, mewing to itself on the rugged floor.

The state of emergency that had been decreed in the country now for about a month since the coup attempt had been revoked. But the night curfew was still on. At first, movement during the night was strictly forbidden to all persons and only the military officials were allowed to patrol the streets for the sake of peace. Now the Chef had in a typical one man show reduced the curfew's time. It was no longer for the whole night but movement from 10:00 pm and above was forbidden. God alone knew what these soldiers were doing in the streets. They were notorious for burglaries

112

into shops which they were called upon to protect. Rapes were no longer news, any woman who ventured out of her house in the night was doing so at her own risk, and she could be raped and let to go if she was lucky or she could be raped and killed or locked up so that she could continue providing free sex. Any woman who was daring enough to refuse the soldiers what was due them was certain of what her fate was. In fact, the streets were a battleground where martial law was total. If you were held up by these soldiers and you happen not to be in possession, of your identification papers, money could do the trick but without money, you were sure never to see you children again.

Yes, these soldiers had absolute freedom, neither their superiors, the law nor their conscience posed any hindrance or problem to them. Homes were broken into with absolute impunity, all you had to do in such a situation was to surrender all the money in your possession or get a treat of the bullet. There were many things you could batter your life for. You could handover money, all of it, property; TV and radio sets most preferable and if you preferred to retain your property you could then hand over your wife or your daughter for the night.

Yes, might is right, few were those who were that daring to venture out in the night. Even thieves had understood the message. Stealing now was carried out mostly during the day; hell was any thief's fate that happened to be caught and refused to share his booty with the soldiers. Even prostitutes had understood the message, there were no prostitutes to be seen by street corners, no matter the money one had. Rendezvous were now arranged in the daytime, only soldiers' call girls could be seen in the streets at night. One prostitute could serve the needs of up to ten soldiers. The pay was a blunt acknowledgement for the service with expressions like; "tu a une borne chaire".

Since the curfew started Newit did not give any room for error, he made sure that he was home by 7:00pm no matter what. If there was anything to be done after that time however important, it must as of necessity be shifted to the next day or some other day.

Diane was now home for about four days. She was so excited to tell Newit everything that happened and the places she visited while in France. Diane felt her level of French had significantly improved.

"Moi je ne parle plus le français du petit-negre Mais le français parisien." Diane was wont to say, whenever anyone challenged her French. Diane talked about her visits to the Alps, the Tour d'Eiffel, La place Parisienne, the Cote D'Azur amongst other places. Whenever she started talking about France, Newit immediately fell asleep and would answer 'uh-huh!' just to keep the conversation going until Diane finally got angry and queried Newit for not paying her attention. Diane brought Newit two gifts from France, one, a polo sweatshirt from her daughter Stephanie and the other a diamond wrist watch that she herself bought. Newit would ask her how Stephanie knew that the sweatshirt was going to fit him and Diane could reply that Newit's framed picture at hung conspicuously at her daughter's Paris V apartment thanks to her initiative..

A week after Diane's return, Newit decided to tell her about Mandala's letter. It was Sunday morning and Newit had decided that he was going to church; Diane had opted to accompany him. Newit also intended to pay a visit to the Brauns before they left for Germany.

"My dear, I forgot to tell you about the letter I received from my son Mandi some two weeks ago." Newit bellowed as he knotted his Italian crossed clubs tie over a dark blue shirt by the dressing table.

"Oh my God, you mean it and what did he say?" Diane asked while slipping on her multicoloured, Kente blouse, hurrying to catch up with Newit. He cleared his throat and while adjusting his non-fused collars.

"He said he wanted to pay me a visit during the holidays," he continued.

"Did his no-nonsense mother accept, um?"

"He had not yet told her, but I believe she has no other option than accepting."

"Hurry up we're almost late, it's already 9:20."

He's welcome anytime." Diane chuckled as she picked up her handbag with one hand and the other, her lip stick, anti-perspirant and a large hair comb then proceeded to the dressing mirror for her daily aesthetic ritual. After about what seemed like an eternity she finished lipsticking, turned towards Newit who was already running out of patience and asked:

"How do I look?" As she topped her hair with a white French lady's hat that was a gift from her youngest daughter as he laughed out of the room.

"You look umh…. terrible, I mean terrific," he joked as he laughed out of the room while Diane called out for him to wait for her.

After church, Newit and Diane both accompanied the Brauns to the mission house which they still occupied. After they had been served some soft drinks by Hilda the oldest of the Brauns seven children, Simon took advantage of the absence of her mother, who was in the kitchen to lean

115

forward behind the settee in which both Newit and Diane were seated to whisper into his ears.

"I don't want to go, but mom says I must, can you help me to stay back?" Newit was startled and was forced to exhibit a broad grin to the consternation of Diane. Simon leant over the settee now and looked Newit straight in the eye and Newit wondered if this was the shy boy he knew.

Newit cleared his throat turned towards Simon and started:

"Son I know how difficult it is for you to leave after such a long time, but just try to forget about Banta for the moment. You're going to meet other friends in Germany, who are better than those you have here, you understand?" Simon blushed and his face turned into disappointing twistings and he cried out:

"I'm not leaving, unless Joel and Che are leaving with me." Her mother heard the voice and immediately came into the sitting room with an expressionless face that had almost turned into a mask since Rev. Braun died.

"You're leaving, now you better go into your room and pack up your dresses." Simon left the sitting room and went outside, disappointed; he wished he could disappear until after his family had left.

Newit, Diane, Helen and her two older children discussed on almost every subject, until they had lunch together for the last time and it was finally time for Newit and Diane to leave. After Helen and her children had walked a little way with them, the moment for parting came. Newit suddenly realized how difficult it was to say goodbye to someone you had known for long.

"Goodbye Helen, we'll all miss you." Diane was by Newit's side and all she could do was to grimace.

116

"Goodbye Newit, we'll equally miss you but I promise to be back to Africa next year." Both Newit and Diane nodded in approval, there was some silence and Simon cut in:

"We have our boys' camp on Thursday, can you beg mom for me to stay back and join them after?"

"Yes my boy, I'll do anything for you but now you have to go back home, I'm inviting you next Christmas, then you'll attend the next camp, umh!"

Newit finally to convince Simon to go with her mother, patted the young man on the back and removed a black box that he was holding in his feeble arms.

"Whao! It's gold, mom look at it". Simon couldn't believe his eyes as he handed the golden watch to his mother. Newit and Diane each embraced the Braun children, thereafter got into their Ford car as the Brauns waved at them excitedly. Newit was happy for one thing that Helen was no longer very disturbed about her husband's death.

It was Christmas, and it was the third year which Diane spent with Newit since they became husband and wife. Christmas this time around fell on a Saturday. The streets were empty safe for those few Christians to whom Christmas meant anything out of merry making. On such a day, the pews of the church were usually filled especially by children. Those parents, to whom church worship meant little, always endeavored to send their children to church as their own representatives. Almost every parent could afford a new dress for his children on this day. There were those parents who waited till the end of the year to be able to afford their children new dresses in order to avoid the scorn of their friends. Children were to be seen inside as well as outside the church exhibiting toys of various kinds. There were some children who disturbed church tranquility by the rattling of their toy guns. Some kids could be heard whistling outside; the girls happily cuddled their toy white babies to the admiration of on-lookers.

There were some Christians, who had afforded new dresses for themselves, but there were still many who were dressed in old clothes because they hadn't the money to buy new ones. There were some Christians who only went to church once a year and that was on Christmas. One could profess any religion even paganism or atheism but celebrated Christmas. This feast was meant for everyone, in fact there was no discrimination as far as its celebration was concerned.

Christmas meant reconciliation, according to Rev. Ntubo, this was the time every Christian should forgive his brother as Christ even in dying begged his father to forgive his murderers for they knew not what they did. This message was further reiterated by the choirs in the church which sang 'Christmas is the time for reconciliation, Christmas is the time of forgiveness'. Newit together with Diane and his nephew Chebi were among the sea of heads that were listening to Rev. Ntubo with such rapt attention that one could be tempted to think that he and not Christ was the way to heaven.

As Newit, Diane and Chebi were coming to church that morning they passed several persons on their way who were already drunk as early as 8:00 am. To these fellows, this was just the beginning of the day; it was such a wonderful way to usher in Christ. Rev Ntubo dwelled at length about the symbolism of Christ's birth.

"Who would have thought that Our God would decide to come into this our sinful world in a simple manger, not in some sophisticated manner, by this very act, God wanted to teach mankind what humility meant. So I often do find it

118

difficult to understand why if our God, who is greater than all, holiest should be able to humble himself to come into our sinful world in the simplest manner, takes on our human form, and is killed in the most despicable and most shameful manner on that cross because of our sake but we are still full of ourselves to accept him. My brothers and sister, I want you to think about that cross, his crucifixion, his death and his resurrection just for your sake. Just because he wants you to come back to him, because he loves you so much so that he doesn't want you die in your disobedience, in your sins".

Back in the streets, there were people who were as prepared as the Christians were to celebrate this great day. For Pa Sweet wine as this cranky looking old man was known, this day was a day to settle scores. This was the day for him to show those rich lads that they were not the only ones who had the right to enjoyment.

"My boy, you see, I have worked for four governors of this province as a yard boy. I have always been a 'boy boy' or by my first name Thomas, in front of my children by my patron's wife when I was still sweeping her yard. But now nobody calls me boy any more, since I retired I am my own 'Patron' now. That means that I have to drink to my fill now, I don't have anybody to answer to. Even on Christmas day when Patron and Madam were out there in the Whiteman country I was always here to wash their clothes, to trim the hedges to dump dirt, to run errands, and had no time to enjoy my beer except in hiding. I have to celebrate this day for that, or don't you think so my son?" Pa sweet wine finally rattled to a stop. Johnnie who had become a regular drinking partner of Pa Sweet wine queried:

"But, you don't have to drown yourself in beer and if that is the reason for celebrating this day."

"I don't have to answer 'sah' or madam again, why should I not drink on Christmas, don't we eat on this day? Let me remind you, Youngman, I did not kill Christ, and if he died to save me, then I have a right to celebrate by drinking, that's how we celebrate funerals." Pa Sweet wine finished his sentence with another gulp of his foul stinking rum that was brewed in the most doubtful manner one could think of. Though Pa Sweet Wine was just forty-nine, 'Ordontol', a locally brewed spirit had made him look like one in his late seventies. Johnnie decided to pick a quarrel with him accusing him that he was a failure and a shame to his family.

"Pa Sweet," as he called out the short form of the older man's name:

"That is how you behaved to your three wives and fifteen children, and they fled you."

"Look here young man, let me tell you this, what goes up must always come down one day, why do you think a dry leaf does not remain in the air? Even if they go, I'm getting married to a young virgin as soon as I get my pension."

They both laughed and Pa Sweet Wine commanded more run for himself and beer for his companion, after all it was Christmas that came once a year. For him spirits were always sweet and he often called spirits Sweet wine.

When Newit, Diane and Chebi left the church at about twelve thirty, the streets were still empty, but preparations were heating up in the neighborhoods for the grown up whose celebrations were meant for the night. Daytime was for children, so that when they were going to bed the grownups would start their own day with no kids to pester them.

Newit and Diane did some visiting in the late afternoon, firstly they visited the Gantas, and also Newit decided that they pay a visit to Mrs. Shuila, his ex- secretary at NUC. They also visited the Memorgas who were Diane's family friends; they finally rounded up their visit at Atebe Lem's place who was a cousin to Diane to meet his recently wedded wife.

Newit had successfully convinced Diane that they should spend Christmas evening together at home unlike in the past, when they had spent it visiting and going out with friends for dinner to as late as 10:00pm. Newit felt that he really needed to be alone with Diane, for she had come to mean everything to him, his only source of hope. He just wanted to forget about the troubles he had gone through and she was the only one who could help him in that regard. She was the embodiments of his sufferings as well as the safe haven that he had always found refuge in. When the world came crumbling on him, she comforted him and even risked her life for him. So Newit decided that this Christmas was dedicated to her.

As Newit went to bed that evening, he could not help but think of the poem, one of the little kids of the Boys Brigade recited in church earlier on that morning whose wordings left an indelible mark on his mind. The poem went thus;

Christ's near
So I can hear the trumpets sounding
The Angels're readying
But am I prepared?
Yes, No, I can't say.

Christ' here
The nation's divided against itself
Friends've turned foes
Rulers, murderers

121

Citizens, rebels.

Christ's here
The world's caught up with itself
The nations' with themselves
Armies, one against another
Disease, hunger 'n' poverty the order
The rich, richer, the poor, poorer.

Christ's everywhere
I'm not lost
The nation's not,
Nor the world.

Christ's hope
Christmas testifies it.

Epilogue

"The country was sick, the medics had said so, the country was mad, the psychiatrists had concluded, the country was condemned to hell, the clergy had intimated, in short the country was not itself. So many people out in the streets, jobs were nowhere to be found, the schools were full with eager hungry children but the teachers were lacking, the hospitals were bursting with patients, yet no doctors. Dirt was everywhere, but who cared to clean it up, people suffocated themselves or were suffocated to death by problems, who bothered? Young men stole small sums of money, old men, big sums, who could catch them. Debts were unbearable but the promise was; "I'll pay." Crime was the order of the day, yet no one could raise an eyebrow. You eat, I eat, if you keep quiet, then I'll do same. Churches increased yet Christians reduced, the sun was hot but the farm had to be worked, rain was unbearable but people had to travel. There was no money, yet one had to buy, there was no hope yet one had to live."

One reporter of a foreign tabloid described this horrible situation in Cameon.

Everywhere one passed round Banta, these were some of the reasons one heard from the protesters who had joined in the revolution. The country for three days now was in turmoil, the young and the old were all in the streets. The shops were all looted, the banks robbed, women raped, hospitals ransacked, drugs stolen, patients abandoned. The police had refused to shoot; the army had become more militant than protesters.

It was rumoured that the Chef was at large, so were his ministers, some had escaped abroad, some to their villages, some hidden in their bunkers, and others still at the marabouts's. Nobody was in charge now; all were in charge, none the boss and none the servant. All were equal now at least for the first time. A cobbler could now command a governor. The guards had all fled the prisons and the prisoners were on the rampage.

There was only one law now and that law, law of action. Intimidations were attempted, men became chicken hearted, children; warriors while women wept and prayed.

Action was spontaneous, people responded to one desire only and that was the desire to see things anew, all that was wanted was change, it did not matter what course this change took in so far as it resulted to the desired end. Tension that had built up the decades rightly or wrongly lacking a medium of expression now had the chance now to manifest.

"Down with the traitors, down with the robbers," these chants were to be heard from weary old faces.

"I'd better die here in the streets than die in my bed when I know my children's future has been siphoned," one middle-aged lady uttered to a reporter in the company of two of his sons.

"We've saying it shouldn't be the same people eating, while the masses seat on their floors waiting for the crumbs from their tables", the lady continued. One farmer said;

"We work seventy hours a week and are paid twenty percent of the hours as if it were a favour those rich thieves do us."

One trade unionist shouted at the top of his voice to a mass of dream-like plantation labourers;

"Nous avons de familles aussi, a nous la liberté", on est des citoyens paisible" "Vive la révolution", so the placards read.

It was reported that intense fighting took place at the residence of the Chef between the rioters and the loyal elements of his private security for two days. His elements finally gave in to the people, not without a price, as many as a hundred of them lost their lives. The guards fought with sophisticated Romanian firearms while the people fought with locally fabricated dane guns, machetes, sticks and stones, spears, bottles and not the least, their months. When they finally broke in the Chef had fled, his wives and children were all in, they were placed under immediate house arrest.

It was rumoured that the chef fled with his private bodyguard in a military helicopter to an unknown destination. With the capitulation of the presidential fortress, parliament followed, the radio and the airport did same. The Chief of the joint staff of the Armed Forces declared for the revolutionists, he called upon all the loyalist forces to surrender and pay allegiance to the new Chef.

No one could say for sure how many people took part in the rebellion, but some estimates put the figures at two hundred thousand. Not less than seven hundred civilians and rebels had lost their lives while the loyalists lost about three hundred.

Defections and renunciations were massive, some government ministers and top officials of the ruling party immediately declared for the new Chef. The government party now had a new leader, those who protested were safely eliminated by their own peers who competed among themselves for allegiance to the new Chef. Garba Mansa's people's Allied Movement wasted no time in declaring their own support; if you hesitated you could pay for it dearly.

Swiss banks trembled, business could be interrupted, accounts could be frozen, clients could be lost. Family relations and friends held their hearts in their mouths, scholarships could be withdrawn, appointments annulled, contracts annihilated.

Yet the drumbeats in the streets rose higher and higher while others wept, others rejoiced, life's drama could never be full comprehended, the nearer you thought you had got there, the further you realized the distance way.

Yes, there was hope and one wish in the streets and that was the wish to be somebody, for tomorrow to be better, for wine to flow, for more bread on tables, for safe neighborhoods, for merit's triumph, for better children, for better schools the list went on and on.

Newit was frightened, though he had wanted change he couldn't say if this was the change he wanted, though Mandala had returned home for holidays as he promised and Diane was still ever present, and an offer for him to take up a vacant lecture position as professor Emeritus of Government at Columbia State University his alma Mata, he still feared for his dear country to which he had returned to so many years ago to serve faithfully.